LYNT

BUT IT'S NOT FAIR
EDITION 2

BUT IT'S NOT FAIR

EDITION 2

ANEETA PREM

www.freedomcharity.org.uk

First published in Great Britain by Prem Publishing

Copyright © Aneeta Prem 2011

Aneeta Prem asserts her moral right to be identified as the author of this work

A catalogue record of this book is available from the British Library

Cover Design by Trident Marketing Anglia Ltd

Illustrations by Kati Teague with Thanks - www.sproggs.com

Set in Avenir

First Published in Great Britain 2011

ISBN Number 978-0-9569751-0-2

Printed and bound in Great Britain by CPI Group (UK) Ltd, Croydon, CR0 4YY

ISBN Number 978-0-9569751-3-3

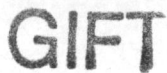

GIFT

DEDICATION

I dedicate this book to the most inspirational being I have ever known,

Author, College Principal, Dad,
Chandra Shekhar Prem
I wish you could have been here to share this.
I miss you every day and I know your love is still with me.

My Darling Mum, Savita Prem
Thank you for being there, not only the Best Mum in the World,
but also for supporting all my ideals and always being there for me.

Vineeta Prem Thornhill, best friend
Beautiful inside and out. A truly enlightened soul!

I have talked about writing this book for a number of years, and in my head, it was finished a long time ago. Finally it's here!

We have come a long way! So many people to thank.

For the wonderful illustrations, Kati Teague, who took a leap of faith to bring the characters to life by drawing beautiful pictures and generously donating her artwork.

And the other wonderful supporters:

Lord Toby Harris Chair of Freedom Charity for his unfaltering support. Sue someone you can count on. Lynne thank you for all the line editing and proof reading. Di and Kim always 'fighting' for Freedom. Anne-Marie Hutchinson OBE for saving so many victims and giving them back hope and their lives. Richard, Frankie and Mits, for their friendship and being 'family.' Rishi 'Darling Nephew 'for being you! William-Tski for your help and believing in the dream. Thank you, Tony, for your support and believing and for sharing the passion.

Vineeta my darling big sister for being as patient with me writing this book as she was when we were kids – you have been a great support. Thanks for reading the characters and sharing the voice.

Thank you Mum for listening to every word I've written and for laughing and crying in the right places and for always being there for me and sharing the journey with me.

And thank you to everyone else who has helped me.

"This is a fantastic book and what this really does is makes this an approachable subject for young people and really highlights that things may be going on in our communities that we don't know about, and the more we know about it the better and that's the role this book should play. Re the assembly, you kept the pupils on the edge of their seats."

Tom Brake MP

"The NAHT urges all schools to include these issues in their PSHE provision and to ensure that the school's workforce is equipped to recognise the signs that there could be potential victims in the school. We are particularly anxious to dispel the view that this is a matter that only affects schools serving diverse communities. NAHT welcomes the lead provided by Freedom and the confidence it gives to schools to recognise that this is essentially a safeguarding matter and that actively opposing these practices should be seen in this light and not an attack on cultural practices."

Russell Hobby,
General Secretary of the NAHT, and Louis Coiffait,
CEO of NAHT Edge, (National Association of Head Teachers)

"The Freedom Charity resource is a very clear and focused approach to two sensitive yet vital subjects and approaches the issues in a balanced, relevant and realistic way. We believe that this resource can form an important part of a planned PSHE programme. The lesson plans can be complemented by the 'But It's Not Fair' book, a fictional account of different perspectives on forced marriages which is available on the Home Office website."

Nick Boddington,
The PSHE Association's Subject Lead

"I think it is very important that schools and young people read this book to understand exactly what is going on."

Keith Vaz MP

"'But It's Not Fair' is an important and brave book, shining light into the dark corner that is forced marriage, and hopefully empowering the friends of young women who are at risk to take action on their behalf.

As a former Member of Parliament, representing in Peterborough, 42 different nationalities of people speaking 91 different languages, I saw at firsthand how mistaken adherence to 'family', 'culture' and 'honour' all too often combined to ruin the futures of bright young women who only wanted a chance to use their education and make their own choices in life. I worked with the local Women's Centre and Women's Refuge to help young women who found themselves in this position and sometimes we succeeded – but all too often, we did not, and yet another girl was sacrificed to the wishes of her male family members.

Now 'But It's Not Fair' is there to alert teachers and friends to the warning signs and there is a greater chance that interventions can be made before it is too late. The book should be essential reading for all young people – and the professionals in every walk of life who have a responsibility and duty help them achieve their ambitions and a future of their own choosing."

Helen Clark,

Associate Director, Royal Public Affairs; MP for Peterborough 1997 – 2005

"I would thoroughly recommend 'But It's Not Fair' to anyone who wants an entertaining but thought-provoking read about forced marriage and why we should all be focusing on the issue. Aneeta led two excellent assemblies at Limehurst Academy in my constituency. The students were clearly engaged and taking on board what she had to say about the work Freedom Charity is doing and their app."

Nicky Morgan MP

"This book was a non-judgmental, fictional account of different perspectives on forced marriages, giving the background to the views of the traditional family and the families arriving to settle in this country. At the same time it showed the horrors of girls of 14 - 16 being taken against their will to India/Pakistan, forced to marry and often being beaten and badly treated by the new husband's family and with little prospect of any contact with their families here. The repercussions on families and school-friends are described, together with ways in which fellow pupils and adults can be alert and know what action they could take. It is a complex situation which requires careful handling. I think the book is essential reading for school children, teachers and all those involved in dealing with the wider situation."

Sheila Eaton,
President National Council of Women

"This book is a fantastic and original resource for students and teachers alike – a must for tackling forced marriage."

Chaz Akoshile,
Joint Head Forced Marriage Unit

Home Office

Foreign &
Commonwealth
Office

And some comments from students who encountered Freedom Charity and 'But It's Not Fair'

Jordon:
"The talk was inspirational as it made me realise just how close to home these issues are and it made me more aware of the issue in its entirety."

Simone:
"I thought it was a very inspirational speech. It's good you're helping people that don't know where to go to."

Daisy:
"I found the assembly very powerful, moving and inspiring and it made me realise how lucky I really am. It was very eye opening and she talked about things I had never even considered."

Callum:
"I thought that the assembly on the Freedom Charity was very informative and quite interesting such as things I didn't know before, for example, boys are also forced into marriage."

Yasmin:
"It's been a great pleasure meeting you today, Your book is amazing! & Very inspirational."

Lea:
"Inspirational to hear what Aneeta is doing."

Yvonne O'Brien:
"Would like to thank you for visiting Westminster University last night. The work you are doing is inspiring and I hope to see Freedom flourish in the future. Wishing you all the success in the world. It was heart wrenching and fascinating."

FOREWORD

BY LYNDA BELLINGHAM

I am so pleased to be writing an introduction to 'But It's Not Fair'. I lived for many years as a victim of domestic violence and it was only the first time that I called the police that I realised there were so many people out there who could help and protect me. I hope this book will make the message clear that Freedom Charity, the police and many other organisations across the country are there to give help and support to those in need.

I discovered when I wrote my own autobiography that a book has a very special way of reaching people. I wrote about my own experiences of a marriage that went horribly wrong, where I was subjected to violence and humiliation, and also about how I recovered from this. I was so touched by the many people who spoke to me or wrote to me about how the book had helped them. Sometimes in these times of social media, Facebook and Twitter, I think we forget that you can still feel very lonely if you have a problem and you feel that you need to keep that problem a secret.

But you can very privately read a book and find comfort and strength from it. A book can be a first step to finding an answer to your problems. I think it is very important that we are aware of all the issues that can make children and young people unsafe and that we do not make the excuse that because we do not understand an issue we can ignore it. For me, Aneeta Prem has made the issue of forced marriage very easy to understand and I think the fact that it is a work of fiction, but based on real life experiences that Aneeta has come across, makes it even more powerful.

I think another great strength of this novel is that it will not only help anyone who may be facing the prospect of a forced marriage, but it will empower those with limited understanding of the issue to reach out and help. My first love in life is being an actress but one of the roles I have cherished is appearing on the ITV chat show 'Loose Women'. I love the show because we talk about all the things that many people are afraid to discuss. I hope that this book opens the door to many discussions all over the country about the issue of forced marriage which is affecting the safety of so many of our young people. I hope the book will help raise awareness and prevent young people being forced into marriage and empower their friends to stop the suffering it causes.

Lynda Bellingham 1948 - 2014,

Lynda, a supporter of Freedom Charity, wrote this foreword for the first edition and we are proud to include it in the second.

"I have been working with women's magazines for over 40 years and to say that I have an understanding of women's issues would be an understatement. I have seen and encouraged women to have equal rights. For over 100 years the publications have provided a wealth of knowledge and understanding. In reading the book 'But It's Not Fair' the reader will gain an insight into the horrendous crime of forced marriage and be equipped to help save not only their best friend's life but will help them understand issues that in the past have been hidden. Young men and women who have been forced into marriage have had their basic human rights torn away from them. The right to have the freedom to choose is essential for both men and women."

Terry Mansfield CBE,

Formerly the Chief Executive of The National Magazine Company which was established in 1910 by William Randolph Hearst, a wholly owned subsidiary of The Hearst Corporation, one of the largest global diversified media companies.

PROLOGUE

SPRING 2010

Last winter a girl from my class went to India with her family to visit relatives. She never came back. Her name was Tara Tally and she was only fourteen.

There was a bit of a fuss surrounding her disappearance. Her friends were questioned by the police, while the rest of us gathered and gossiped in noisy groups in the playground. Eventually it all died down. Everything went back to normal. But, of course, life never went back to normal for Tara. We never saw her again.

Sometimes, when I can't sleep, I think about Tara. I imagine her looking sad and tired, dressed in a sari and sweeping the floor in a small and dusty Indian village.

My sister, Sofia, who's far more romantic than I am, has a different view on what happened. She thinks Tara ran off to star in a Bollywood film and is convinced we'll see her in a movie any day soon: '…looking stunning, starring opposite some utter hunk, singing, dancing and twirling in a silver spangled sari.'

I'm fifteen now and my crazy sister is ten. Sofia's the opposite of me in every way except our looks; she's loud, uninhibited and excitable. We can't help but love her even when she's driving us mad.

Our mum and dad are called Jasmine and Shekhar. They're pretty cool and liberal, especially for Asian parents. Even before they came to England Dad was always very outspoken about politics and just about anything really.

Sofia's favourite saying is, 'But it's not fair.' She says it so often, it's become a family joke and we just smile in response.

I've learned this past year that there's a lot more that's unfair in life than she could possibly imagine in her tiny, ten-year-old head. Before Tara went missing, just like Sofia, my idea of what wasn't fair was not getting what I wanted from the shops or not being able to stay up late, but now I know differently. There's a whole lot more unfair stuff going on in the world, and sometimes it happens to people we know.

1

Wow, it's bling, bling everywhere you look and Sofia is bouncing up and down in excitement and shouting in my ear.

'Vinny, I need a pair of sunglasses to dim the glare from Shah Aunty's gold. Look, she's got about twenty-six gold chains, hundreds of flashing bangles and a dazzling diamond nose ring!' She turns to Mum. 'What does she do about her bogeys if she has a snotty nose?' she asks in her fake-polite voice.

'She blows it,' Mum answers in her stop-being-silly voice.

'Yes but the bogeys must get caught on the butterfly of her nosey,' Sofia says chuckling. Mum sighs and looks away, clearly hoping that ignoring Sofia will shut her up. This never works with my sister. She opens her mouth to ask another question when she's interrupted by Shah Aunty rushing up to Mum, embracing her then pulling her over to a huddle of chattering ladies.

'You look lovely Jasmine…' I hear as Shah Aunty's voice trails away.

It was just six weeks ago that the Shahs sent us a box of ambala ludos – they're those golf-ball shaped orange Indian sweets – and an invitation to Sasha's wedding.

Sasha Shah is eighteen and works in a bank. She's very pretty, quite tall and has sleek, long black hair. Sofia reckons they're extensions; me, I hadn't even thought about it – I'm not interested in that girly stuff.

Shah Aunty isn't really our aunty, but our families are close friends. Sofia and I adore Sasha. She's great fun – laughs a lot – but she's quite homely too and loves to spend her time in the kitchen with Shah Aunty, chatting and flipping through magazines as her mum cooks.

Sasha wears the latest fashions and buys all the latest celebrity and bridal magazines. She often gives us her copies of *Hello* and *OK!*, but Sofia gets annoyed as they're full of holes where Sasha has cut out pictures of hairstyles she likes or outfits she wants to buy. Sofia thinks Sasha always looks amazing but I'm not so sure. It all seems too over the top to me, like she's trying to wear too many styles at once, but what do I know!

She's marrying Jaan. He's from Leicester and I've only met him once before. I've never been to Leicester though. The furthest our family has been is a day-trip to Southend beach and funfair.

The wedding is like a day-trip for us, it's in the countryside at a place called Ongar – it's about an hour away but it's so green and leafy it feels a million miles away from the East End.

Of course we were all very excited about the wedding despite the fact that Mum was making Sofia and me wear the same dress. Sofia wailed about it to anyone who would listen. 'I can't believe we both have to wear a hideous burgundy and white flowery dress. Even though I'm thin and small and Vinny's a tall lanky loon, we're expected to look our best in the same vile dress.' It occurred to me that I should be complaining as I'm the eldest but I'm just not that bothered. The main reason Sofia is seething, however, is because the burgundy and white number looks better on me than her so, as usual, she stamped her foot and shouted, 'But it's not fair!'

Mum does look lovely, I think, as I watch her laugh with the women Shah Aunty has introduced her to. She's dressed in a burgundy sari covered with silver sequins. She looks like a Bollywood movie star.

'We're so co-ordinated and looking like we've hired a stylist to "do" us; we could feature on one of those makeover programmes, but of course we're the "after" not the "before",' Sofia babbles away. 'Everyone is probably jealously sick and pointing to the beautiful family in burgundy who're doing their own dazzling at this wedding,' she whispers excitedly to Dad who is looking very handsome in a black Marks and Spencer suit, a pale blue shirt and burgundy tie. Dad smiles and puts his arm around Sofia. He rarely gets annoyed with her; he just finds her amusing. Mostly I do too but sometimes, ooh, I really could slap her. I never do, of course.

Sofia is always demanding to be the centre of attention, which thankfully takes the heat off me.

The star of the show, though, is definitely Sasha, just as it should be. She's wearing a beautiful, bright red langa. Draped elegantly over her face is a matching veil, glittering with gold sequins, and she's covered in dazzling gold jewellery. She's like an immaculate, life-size doll next to her new husband who is like a magazine model in his cream silk suit. They really do look the perfect couple.

We're standing in the Shah's house and Sasha and Jaan have just been married. It was so quick and easy. She said 'Yes' three times, he said the same, there were some religious readings and then, simple as that, they were married. Cheering, clapping and the flashing of cameras ensued while Shah Aunty bustled around beaming proudly and introducing guests. Now we're about to make our way out of the house to pile into cars for the short drive to the reception.

We arrive at a very plush country-house hotel. In an entrance hall full of scary-looking armour, a lady in a black skirt and white blouse greets us with sugar-rimmed glasses of mocktails decorated with umbrellas and strawberries. I grasp mine as we're ushered into an impressive hall decorated with crimson and gold balloons. Garlands of flowers are draped lavishly from the chandelier. It looks like a red and gold themed film set. Sofia rushes eagerly ahead, hoping to find a seat next to the bride and groom.

'There is a table plan you know, you can't sit anywhere you like,' I whisper as I catch up with her and grab onto her arm. 'Here it is. Look, we're on table five.'

In keeping with the theme, the chairs are gold and the tablecloths deep red. Flower petals, tinsel and confetti decorate the tables.

'Wow, this is like a proper celebrity wedding. Take loads of photos of me for your Facebook page,' Sofia demands. 'My wedding will be just like this, but everyone will have to wear purple,' she sighs. Thankfully, no one is listening, they're too busy jostling to find their seats, eager to begin the feeding frenzy.

2

The wedding banquet is served on gold platters piled high with typical Indian wedding fare. Fried samosas, pakoras, paneer and bright orange chicken tikka are already on the table. The delicious feast continues as our plates are cleared and the waiters reappear with the next course: saffron rice, chickpeas, Bombay potatoes, lamb meatballs, raita, lentil dhal and naan bread.

The room falls silent as we devour the food and I think back to the day we visited the Shahs' house to hear all about the wedding plans. Everyone was really excited. Sasha kept blushing whenever anyone mentioned her fiancé Jaan so we guessed she must be happy about the arrangement. Of course it was Sasha's Aunty Jessie who introduced them. The Shahs met with Jaan's family, then he went to the Shah house for tea. Aunty Jessie is like a matchmaker. Dad thinks she's a bit of a nosy parker, because she's always introducing people to get married. But it has to be admitted, Aunty Jessie has a pretty good success rate in matchmaking.

Finally, we're all full up and the feast's remains are abandoned as the guests stand up, chatting happily as we all wait for the dancing to begin. Sofia moves next to me.

'Why didn't Sasha choose her own husband? Lazy old thing, getting Aunty Jessie to do it,' she says, too loudly I think.

'Shush, Sofia,' I hiss. But it's as if Aunty Jessie heard Sofia, as just at that moment, she turns to look at us and calls to Sofia, 'Why are you spoiling your pretty face by scowling?' before turning back

to the crowd of women that has gathered around her.

Unfazed, Sofia is her usual nosy curious self and wanders over to find out what's going on. Left alone, I have no choice but to follow her.

With their plump bodies wrapped in saris of every imaginable colour, the women around Aunty Jessie look like a bunch of fat, silky peacocks. Sofia and I listen to her boast about the wedding match. The women press forward eagerly.

'I don't know what they would have done without me.' Aunty Jessie shakes her head sorrowfully at the thought. The plump ladies sigh and move their heads along with her. 'Sasha had seen seven possible suitors over the past eight months,' she continues, then she lowers her voice to a whisper. 'Three rejected her, and she said "no way" four times. But I never gave up.' Aunt Jessie smiles. 'I just knew I could find the right husband for her.' Their eyes follow Aunty Jessie's finger pointing to where the bride and groom are sitting on their bridal thrones. It is just at the bit in the wedding celebrations where the bride has to feed her new husband an ambala ludo. Poor Jaan looks as though he is about to gag and choke to death, but he tries his best to smile, chew and swallow while everyone cheers. In the midst of everyone's laughter I notice Sasha wink at him and he whispers something to her that makes her turn as red as her langa. I feel myself blushing too just wondering what they are talking about.

Aunty Jessie holds her arm towards the couple in triumph. 'And look, see how handsome he is, how much in love they are!' The ladies smile and sigh again.

I agree with Sofia though, it's kind of old fashioned that someone as cool and modern as Sasha would let a matchmaker choose her husband. Still, as Dad says, everyone is different and some families are more traditional than ours.

Sasha had asked me to be with her when she met Jaan for the first time, to see if I agreed that he was good enough to marry, but I had a lot of study to do at the time so couldn't go.

Sofia was outraged that she didn't get an invite.

'I can't believe she didn't ask me, doesn't she know that I'm completely up with what's hot and what's not!' she moaned. 'And I'm not even allowed to go around and have a look at him, 'cos you've got homework and Mum and Dad are pretending they're too busy to take me.'

So neither of us got to see Sasha's dream man before she agreed to marry him but she liked him so much at that first meeting that she said she really didn't mind.

When we did finally meet Jaan I thought he was a great guy though I was too shy to talk to him.

'This is my good friend Vinny,' said Sasha, beaming at us both.

'Hi,' I mumbled, in awe of his film-star looks. Sofia was impressed too.

'He's not bad looking for a boy,' she whispered loudly to me. Most of all she was impressed that he had a two-seater sports car and an iPhone. 'Wow, you've got an iPhone,' she said in her sweetest voice as she held her hand out for Jaan to let her have a look.

'Yes,' Jaan replied, smiling. His teeth were so blindingly white, he must have had them whitened.

'What apps have you downloaded?' she asked, trying to impress Jaan as he passed her the phone.

'I love the Maps, look, it shows you where we are.' Jaan pointed to the screen.

'You've got loads of games on here too, can I play?' she pleaded, using her best puppy dog eyes.

'Yes, of course,' he replied as he walked over to Sasha who had told us to come to the kitchen for a drink. 'I'll come and get it off you later. Oh, don't answer any of my calls though,' he said rather forcefully.

Jaan let her play with his phone for over an hour.

'He's really cool, he knows how to wow a girl,' Sofia told me later.

3

It's now time for the aunties and uncles to form a queue to give the happy couple their blessing and to circle Sasha's and Jaan's heads with money before placing it on their laps. Sofia rushes up with five pounds for each of them and, in typical annoying Sofia style, waves her fivers several times around their heads and even once under their noses, but they just laugh and playfully swat her away.

As the guests continue to bless the couple, I watch as Sasha and Jaan gaze into each other's eyes as if there is no one else in the room. They must really be in love though it's hard to believe Aunty Jessie could make that happen! Dad said that Aunty Jessie's matchmaking method is to keep arranging viewings and eventually she hits the jackpot, or – and he laughed at this thought – 'Maybe she just wears everyone down and they eventually agree to a match.' I think Aunty Jessie's one aim in life is to get everyone in the human race married. Sofia returns and nudges me out of my daze.

'If it were me,' she remarks with a sly grin, 'I would be counting all my money. There must be millions of pounds in their laps by now.'

I realise that Aunty Jessie has noticed us standing and watching the happy couple. She laughs as she reaches over to pinch Sofia's cheeks.

'So my darling Sofia, your Aunty Jessie will find a prince for you before long? Should he be fat or thin, light or dark, rich or poor?' I imagine myself as small as possible so she won't start on me too. It's so embarrassing. Some boys are standing nearby and I'm certain they're listening. Please don't say anything to me about husbands, I pray silently.

'No, Aunty, I will choose my own husband,' Sofia announces proudly. And all the ladies laugh.

I can see Sofia is wild about them laughing at her so I drag her away from the group before she says something rude.

'Ha, what do those old ladies know? They don't know me. To them I'm just some little girl,' she shouts as I push her towards an empty corner. 'Aunty Jessie would need several years to prowl the whole planet to find someone good enough to marry me. I know thousands and thousands of boys have probably already told Aunty Jessie that they are desperate to go out with me, why wouldn't they, I'm gorgeous. But I don't really need any help or any introduction, I already have a queue of boys who want to be my boyfriend. I'm a good catch.'

'Oh Sofia, calm down and stop exaggerating, I...' Before I can finish, she stomps off. I'm left standing alone, not caring that she's an embarrassing little brat at times, but just grateful to have escaped Aunty Jessie's husband questions. I don't want to think about such things for a long, long time. Besides, there's school and college first and most importantly, time to just have fun. Boys can definitely wait as far as I'm concerned. Sofia, on the other hand, at just ten years old, has already planned her fantasy wedding day. 'I don't want a traditional Indian wedding,' she'll say. 'My dream wedding is me in a fairytale ballerina dress, with millions and zillions of sequins sewn on by an army of people madly stitching for weeks and weeks. It will have a sweetheart neckline and be fluffy with a train one hundred metres long.'

Sofia is such a kid still, she thinks being married is all about the wedding day and forgets it's really about the wedding being the first day of the rest of your life.

I look about for my friends. The party is going strong; everyone is dancing and having fun, even the older people. Pushing my way through the dance floor I find Sara who is giggling and whispering behind her hand and looking at boys with the other girls our age.

'Isn't Sasha beautiful!' Sara gasps when she sees me. 'They are so much in love.' I laugh and nudge her. I can't believe these girls; they just can't get enough romance out of the occasion!

I spot Sofia, who has obviously forgotten being laughed at, as she's now slap bang in the middle of the dance floor. She loves Bangra music, she knows she's not the best dancer but watching and copying the other guests, she's freestyling, screwing and unscrewing the light bulbs, like the best of them.

'Fancy a dance?' I hear Davey say to Sofia. He's Sasha's gormless, weedy cousin.

'In your dreams,' says Sofia, grabbing his arm and twisting it behind his back.

'Ouch, how did you learn to do that! Come on, let's have a dance,' Davey pleads.

'Come back when you're older,' she says, releasing his arm. She sees me watching her and I shake my head at her in warning. 'What?' she shrugs and gestures all innocently.

I smell Sasha's fragrance before I see her. I turn to greet her and we hug tightly.

'Sasha, you look so happy.'

'He's so lovely, isn't he?' Sasha beams at me. 'He's just told me we're flying off to St Lucia tomorrow! Only two weeks ago I showed him a magazine article on the top ten places in the world to honeymoon and he's booked it as a surprise honeymoon present.'

'Wow, he's such a dream. Ahh,' I put my hand to my forehead and pretend to swoon, Bollywood-style.

'It's an all-inclusive resort. You know you don't have to pay for a thing. Oh I just can't wait, he said he's even bought me a D&G bikini.'

'Wow, can I come?' interrupts Sofia brightly. We ignore her and she goes off muttering something about asking Jaan.

'I feel so lucky, I hope you are as lucky as me when your time comes. You know he's got a younger brother?' Sasha teases.

'No way, I'm not ready to get married, don't think I ever will be.' I won't admit it to Sasha but just the thought of anything to do with boyfriends makes me feel shy and awkward.

'We all say that, but one day, it will happen to you,' Sasha smiles giving me another warm hug.

The party is really starting to heat up when suddenly Mum appears and tells us we have to leave. Dad has some work to do the next day and wants an early start.

Sofia is still in the middle of the Bangra and whines, calling Mum a killjoy.

'It's not fair. There's no democracy in our family,' she says stomping her feet. But Mum stands firm.

'Come on, the cab is waiting outside,' she says as she pushes Sofia through the crowd and towards the exit.

'Everyone is so very sad that we are going so frightfully early,' wails Sofia dramatically. Dad is already saying goodbye to Aunty Shah when we find him.

'The girls are tired and Shekhar has work to do tomorrow,' Mum says, 'and it's a bit of a drive from here back to East London.'

'No I'm not, please let's stay, Mum. It's not fair. No one else is going. Please let's stay just five more minutes,' Sofia pleads. She kind of gets her way in the end as with all the hugs and kisses goodbye, it takes twenty-five minutes to escape.

4

Dad gets in the front of the cab. Sofia begs to sit in the front instead of Dad but she quickly gives in. I think she'd sooner sprawl out over Mum and me in the back, as really she's tired despite protesting that she's not.

'What a nice wedding,' I say, yawning.

'Yes, so perfect and everything so beautiful,' Mum agrees. 'I'm sure they'll be very happy together,' she says hopefully.

'My wedding will be even better than Sasha's; I'm going to marry a prince. Of course you will all need a makeover, but it can be arranged.' Sofia's prattling on again about her dream wedding day. 'The photographs will be in *Hello* magazine, *after* there has been a bidding war of course. All my guests will wear purple, with a white flower…' Bored of her chatter, I tut and close my eyes.

The taxi driver, a friendly looking guy of about Dad's age, turns to smile at her. Sofia misreads his expression and thinks that he's impressed.

'You must come too,' she says, beaming at him. 'It will be a big do, you know.' Dad starts talking to the driver; they're not really listening to her. 'I *am* marrying a prince,' Sofia announces loudly and then just as suddenly closes her eyes. I open my eyes.

'You'll have to kiss a lot of frogs first,' I mutter grumpily, but Sofia is already asleep. I wish it were as easy for me to fall asleep, but it's hard without anyone to lean on.

'So your daughter is marrying a prince, eh?' I overhear the taxi driver asking Dad.

Dad laughs. 'No, no, only in her sweetest dreams.'

'But you have found husbands for your daughters, no?' he enquires, more seriously.

'Well, they need to finish school first, then there's university and getting a job before they find their prince, I'm sure,' Dad says, very matter-of-fact.

'They will choose, you will not decide for them?' the taxi driver asks, briefly turning to Dad with a shocked expression. I listen and watch under nearly closed eyelids from the back seat, pretending to be asleep.

Now I'm less interested in sleeping and I listen intently, hoping no one notices I haven't fallen asleep.

Mum sits silently, unaware I am listening and seems relieved Dad is trying to get the taxi driver to see the error of his ways.

'My daughters will marry who I say,' declares the driver when Dad says nothing. 'After all, I know what's best for them, what do girls know?' He taps the steering wheel as he speaks.

'And your daughters,' Dad asks gently, 'what do they want?'

'They want what I want. Listen, our children are being corrupted by the West; no manners, no morals. It's our job to protect them, you must agree?' Dad stays quiet, letting him finish. 'When my daughter Fatima turns fifteen, I will take her home. It has already been decided. She will marry my brother's son; he is a good boy, training to be a car mechanic. They will live with my brother back home for a year or so, then I will bring them both back to the UK. You see, everything will be fine.'

'How old is your brother's son?' Dad asks.

'He must be about twenty-five, twenty-six. He's a good boy. It was decided over ten years ago that they would marry. We are a close family. It has all been decided.' He beams at Dad and turns to look at me as he stops at the traffic lights.

Dad slows his voice down and speaks even more quietly while keeping a smile on his face. I've noticed it's a technique he uses to get someone to really listen.

'And, if they don't want to marry? Your daughter is very

young, too young for marriage. And too young to be sent to another country especially if it is against her will. Let her get a good education then allow her to decide, ask her what she wants. There's no point in forcing them,' Dad reasons.

'No, my brother said that once they get an education, that is it. They are spoiled, they won't listen to us, they become too independent. I know what is best for my girls, they will do as I say. Anyway, they would not want to bring shame on our family. How could I look my brother in the eye, hold my head up, if she refused to do what I say? No, no, it would be impossible.'

'What does your wife say?' Dad's tone has hardened. 'What do your daughters think about all this?'

'What can they say? I am the head of the family. Listen my brother, take your daughters in hand now.' He glances in his rear view mirror and sees me watching him. I don't even try to hide my shock and displeasure. He shakes his head.

'Your honour is all you have,' he tells Dad, but I know he is directing it at me too.

'No, I'm afraid I don't agree with you my friend. The love of my family is what I have. Women are to be treasured, cherished. All I want is for my children to be happy. Their happiness is our happiness,' Dad impresses on him.

'All well and good, brother, but you don't want your daughters to marry a gora or a karla do you?' the driver says, almost spitting out the words.

Dad has spent his entire life fighting injustice and so far has been going easy on the taxi driver. Fortunately for the driver, we arrive at our flat just as Dad is gearing up to give him the lecture of his life.

So instead, Dad patiently and quietly pays the driver while Mum wakes Sofia and ushers us towards our flat. Before he closes his door, Dad leans back into the car and I hear him say one final thing to the driver. 'My friend, please don't force your daughters into doing anything that will cause them pain.' I never hear a response. Dad closes the door and the conversation is over.

As we struggle into our pyjamas and slip under the bed covers, Sofia babbles excitedly about the wedding again. I am silent, but my mind is racing. If I were that driver's daughter, Fatima, right now he would be making arrangements to marry me off to some man I didn't know, didn't love and who was at least ten years older than me.

Mum shouts from the other room: 'Quiet Sofia, get to sleep now.' And Sofia, surprisingly obedient for once, falls fast asleep. I shiver and turn over in bed, trying to get warm, but I'm chilled to the bone and feel wide awake. I lie flat on my back and stare at the ceiling, imagining how different my life could be.

Sofia's right, life isn't fair but in a far worse way than she can imagine. I realise how much freedom I have while some of my friends at school probably face a future much like Fatima's. I start to wonder again about Tara who went on holiday to India and never came back.

5

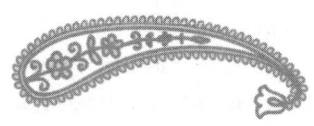

The Saturday after the wedding is a typical, quiet weekend afternoon in our house. No bling today.

Dad has finished all his chores and fallen asleep. Now Mum is heading off for her usual nap and I can see Sofia thinks she's forgotten about homework, but no, she turns to remind Sofia to do it now. I suppress a giggle.

'Oh Mum,' she groans, 'homework is such a bore. A whole week at school, finally it's the weekend and I still have to do work. It's not fair.' But Mum has already gone. 'Please do it for me,' she begs me.

'Why can't you do it yourself?' I say, looking at her homework diary.

'I just can't. I don't know what to write. You're so clever at that sort of thing. Stupid Miss wanted us to write about ourselves this year. She says it's good practice as we are now in year six students. And when I said, "Do we have to, Miss?" she said I should be able to write tons as I don't ever stop talking about myself. What a cheek!'

I laugh. 'All right, I'll help you.' Sofia's face breaks into a massive smile. She's too daft to realise I've given in too easily. 'Yes, I will start with what a noisy little brat you are. Oh, and how you are too lazy to do your own homework and I'll write how you...'

'You wouldn't dare!' she squeals.

'Just you try me sis. Now go on, have a go at it and I'll help you if you get stuck. You have done tons already at school.'

'You're supposed to be my best friend,' she whines as I go back to reading my magazine.

Sofia's been working on her autobiography project all this year and brings it home most weekends to work on. As she throws down her pen and goes to the kitchen, probably in search of a snack, I sneak over to read what she's done.

So here goes, all about me, me, me…

I'm 10. I'm not a heart-stopping beauty but I will be. I have lovely shiny golden brown skin. My hair is so long if I'm not careful it could end up wet when I go to the loo, it's almost to my waist.

I am going to be a better-looking version of Princess Catherine of Cambridge or even Aishwarya Rai. She's my favourite Asian superstar. And I expect I'll have Hollywood superstars fighting over me. I'll be on TV flicking my hair and saying "Because I'm worth it." I'll be caught on camera by all the paparazzi desperate to get me on the front cover of every magazine.

I don't tell lies. I tell stories and sometimes (well mostly) I add on a bit to make them more interesting. There is a thin line between truth and lies. But embellishing a story isn't lying! (I looked embellishing up Miss!)

I was born in a London hospital. The only good thing about being born in Bethnal Green is that I am a real live cockney 'cos I was born within the sound of Bow Bells. I'm dead proud of that. I make my cockney accent heavier than it really is as it's so cool. My big sister Vinny doesn't have a cockney accent, she talks dead proper English like our parents.

While Mum carried me in her tummy my sister Vinny was asked by Dad and Mum's friends if she wanted a baby brother or sister. My Dad and Mum wanted a baby brother to make the family complete and for Dad. Oh and someone to take care of Mum and Dad in their old age. As Indians it's our duty to take care of our parents as they took care of us and made all those sacrifices for us. (Though I think this isn't fair as we didn't ask to be born.)

So Vinny would say she wanted a baby sister so she could dress me up like a baby doll. Vinny didn't know any boys and I think she was a bit scared of them. She prayed every night for a baby sister to play with. Mum and Dad were upset and wanted her to change her prayers to asking for a brother.

Mum was sad that she gave birth to a daughter. Dad told her not to be so silly. It didn't make any difference. Mum said that if we lived in India she would have had another try because that was easy as they had tons of servants in India. And I must have guessed all this because from before I can remember I tried to be like a real son. Tough and loud.

I'm pleased because my Mum who is called Jasmine is still really young and pretty. She cooks great food and after she finishes work on Saturdays at around 1 o'clock, she stops off to buy bread from the bakery and it's usually still hot. We rush around her and dive in trying to pick bits off but she waves her arms around and cuts the bread into really thick slices and puts loads of butter on that melts instantly. It's our weekly treat and we scoff the lot. She might bring home cakes too or bread pudding or apple pies. They're not as good as next-door-aunty's but they're still welcome. We wish we could have hot bread every day but next-door-aunty says it's bad for us to eat really hot bread as it will give us all tummy ache. It's not fair to tell such fibs! We never get tummy ache no matter how much hot bread we eat. Adults are always saying these things. Always warning us about things that never happen. They don't know as much as they say they do.

I'm not supposed to but when I get home from school I go to see next-door-aunty and she makes me tea. She's the best cook in the world apart from Dad and Mum. She makes tons of great stuff to eat. Eggs and chips, stews, cakes and roast dinners. Vinny and I love

her cooking. It isn't spicy, quite plain really, but better than school dinners.

Next-door-aunty lives alone. Mum and Dad have kind of adopted her as our Gran. I've never met my real Gran but next-door-aunty will do just fine for now.

Her name is Grace Dawn. Her poor old husband died soon after they were married. We don't really talk about him much. I always tap on her kitchen window and peer through to see if she's got any chips on the go. I shout, "Oooh oooh Aunty shall I come in?" She loves my company and all my stories. Dad says she's really lonely so she's lucky we moved in next door to her. Mum grumbles that she spends more time in our flat than her own. I wish I could call her Granny but from when I was little I've always said next-door-aunty so it seems odd to change now.

She pops over every night at around 7 o'clock so Mum has a chance to get in and put the dinner on. Then the landing is full of the smell of our tea and all of the neighbours know what we are eating. Some of them don't like it much but I don't care, except when Mum cooks saag (spinach and mustard leaves that are boiled for hours in the noisy pressure cooker). Then it just pongs and the taste is worse than boiled bogeys. My big sister Vinny pretends to love the torturous saag. She says yum how lovely, Mummy.

My Mum's Mum died when she was small so Mum didn't really learn how to do mum things. She never reads us stories and never makes fairy cakes though she does make great fake eggy bread with **besan** which is chickpea flour instead of eggs. She makes great onion omelettes too. They're a bit smelly on your breath. But hot onion omelette on white bread with Heinz tomato ketchup and mmm, I'm in heaven. On Sunday she fries bread and dips it in sugary milky stuff that's so yummy even though it looks soggy. We sit like baby birds squawking for more.

Vinny is five years older than me and she is a right goody two shoes. She can cook whole meals from scratch and she can even make round rotis. She's Mum's favourite because she's good and sweet and never shouts or screams or yells like I do. Vinny is very pretty. She's like an older version of me but a bit more filled out in the right places. She's very clever and she loves reading. She's a swot bag. I hate reading so Vinny has to read to me. She reads the classics like 'Lady Chatterley's Lover'. I make her read any rude bits over and over again. Everyone is proud of perfect Vinny. She doesn't mind playing games with me and normally lets me win too. She's dead good at card tricks. And she knows some really good jokes. Some are a little rude and I love those best.

I have to share a bedroom with Vinny. I don't mind really. We talk late into the night with Vinny reading me bedtime stories though Mum sometimes gets cross when she hears me roaring with laughter or practising my opera singing. I could easily be an opera super star. I have a great voice so I don't understand why everyone tells me to pipe down!

We live on the third floor of the white flats opposite the railway arches in Bethnal Green which is in East London. We don't have designer clothes, just High Street stuff and too many of our outfits are identical. I hate that. I want to look like me not a mini-me version of Vinny. I moan and plead with Mum to let me have my own style like Sasha does but clothes are a problem anyway as I am too thin for anything to fit.

My Mum and Dad aren't like other mums and dads. They work all the time and Mum even works on Saturday mornings. I suspect it's because it gets her off doing the housework. Dad does all that. He drags us to Tesco to do the weekly shop then lets us choose a treat at least. Then we walk down to the market stalls and get food from the fruit and veg guy and toilet rolls from another.

When we get home Vinny puts the shopping away and I get to hoover. I love hoovering 'cos I get to practise my opera singing. I think I could shatter a glass if I sing even louder. I want to go on the X-Factor. Vinny calls it the Z-Factor so I sing louder to annoy her.

Mum gets home from sewing on a machine in a shoe factory all morning and she's also an Avon lady except she never goes out and ding dongs. She only shows the Avon book to her friends at work. When the big Avon box comes Vinny and I love to check it out. I love to sneak a squirt of this or a dab of that. Once Mum even won a beauty contest as the most beautiful Avon lady. She had a sari on and she had a sash with diamonds on it and I was really proud of my beautiful glamorous Mum. She looked like a model (well a five foot three model).

On school days Dad always rushes straight home from his translating work at the Council as fast as he can to be with us. He normally gets home by 5.30. From the time Vinny and I get home from school we've usually turned the house into a tip.

When it's nearly 5.30 I stand on the worktop in the kitchen and look out of the kitchen window, pulling at the net curtains to see out and I can see Dad as he comes into view under the arches. Vinny and I run around frantically and tidy up and get out of our school uniform as Mum says we have to change as soon as we get home from school.

On Friday nights to celebrate the weekend Dad buys us Kit Kats as a treat. He loves Kit Kats but Turkish Delights are his favourite. He rarely buys them though because they are much dearer.

Dad is super cool. He has a huge fan club outside the family as well. He's great at sorting out people's problems. Not like some soppy agony aunt. He's more like a super hero. He never wears his underpants on the outside of his trousers of course. That would just *be silly. But he's a super hero none the less.*

My Dad isn't like other dads and he tells great stories about his life. I think I've got his genes for exaggerating stories. But maybe he is telling the whole truth. Who knows.

Sofia comes back with a plate of biscuits and I leap back on to the sofa. I don't think she noticed me reading her work. The house is quiet as our parents are still napping. We're not allowed to have the TV on so I challenge her to a card game of Snap.

Although Sofia has exaggerated the truth about Dad in her project, there are times when Dad has helped resolve all sorts of problems and people are always asking him for advice. One thing's for sure about Dad, he knows how to fix things.

I'm surprised we didn't wake our parents with all Sofia's whingeing whenever she lost at Snap. It was the doorbell that woke them and Mum came into the living room smoothing down her hair.

'Sofia put away your homework and answer the door, your Aunties are here.'

'Yes!' and 'No! All at the same time!' shrieks Sofia. This is the highlight of her week, Saturday night, when we all watch Britain's Got Talent. 'Worst luck, tonight the Aunties will be here and they talk, a LOT.'

Next-door-aunty is already at the door too having heard Shah Aunty and Aunty Jessie knocking. They aren't our real aunties of course, but anyone more than ten years older than me is known fondly as an aunt. We rarely see our real ones as they all live in India.

As they bustle through the door, already chatting and laughing loudly, Sofia races ahead of them and dives onto the sofa before they can take up all the space with their 'big fat bottoms' as Sofia always says rudely. She turns the volume up full blast and hides the remote control under her leg. She's so obvious, my sister.

'Please turn it down, we can't hear ourselves think,' Mum moans.

'But Mum,' she shouts, 'I can't find the remote.'

'Turn it down just a little, darling,' Dad reasons, finding the remote and hiding it from her.

'But Aunty wants to watch it, don't you Aunty?' she looks pleadingly at next-door-aunty. Next-door-aunty smiles blankly at Sofia She doesn't know what's been going on and turns back to listen to Aunty Jessie who is banging on at next-door-aunty about what a great matchmaker she is.

'You know, Mrs Swan, you are a handsome woman. It's a shame to be alone, let me take down some details, and I am sure I can find you a nice young man. How about an Asian man?' Aunty Jessie nudges next-door-aunty gently. I'm pretty sure her offer's genuine.

'Get off with you, I'm too old to bother with all that at my age.' Next-door-aunty roars with laughter.

'I know lots of men, widowers who would love a new wife and would suit you well. Please let's sort out a date or two.' Aunty Jessie isn't giving up.

'No, I am not getting involved with that forced marriage lark. I've read about it in the paper you know. Oh no, no one would get me into that, it's barbaric, it is,' next–door-aunty says teasing Aunty Jessie.

'My dear Mrs Swan, we are talking about a discreet introduction. You are mistaking arranged marriage with forced marriage,' Aunty Jessie says, going bright red.

'Well I don't care what you call it, I don't want some lazy good for nothing man in my life, not at my age.'

Aunty Jessie looks shocked at the outburst. It looks like next-door-aunty has broken a record; she's the only person in known history to get Aunty Jessie to back off.

Coughing, Shah Aunty interrupts the tension.

'You have no idea how many suitors we showed to our dear Sasha,' Shah Aunty boasts, swiftly bringing the focus of the evening back to Sasha's wedding.

'I know, I showed her at least ten of my best boys,' Aunty Jessie sighs.

'You said seven last time you told that story,' I pipe in remembering what she said at the wedding, but no one pays me any attention.

'Yes, yes, but finally she met the right one,' Shah Aunty says looking as if she's about to start praying. 'I don't know what I would have done if we had to go and meet another ten boys while she was being so fussy.'

I was fuming and was so riled inside, I wished I had the guts to say what I was thinking:

'Sasha wasn't choosing a pair of shoes you know; it was the man she would hopefully spend the rest of her life with.'

'I knew she would fall for Jaan, how could she not? She loved him the moment she saw him,' Aunty Jessie gushes. 'Speaking of weddings, have you met the new family who's moved in? I hear that one of their daughters has just returned to their home village to marry…' My ears prick up.

'Do they have any other children?' I ask, keen to have a new friend nearby.

'Yes, lots of children I hear and one your age I think.' Happy with that answer I turn back to look at the TV.

'This is such trash TV, they can't even sing,' I complain.

'They are very smart-looking boys though,' Shah Aunty says.

'It's all about looks Aunty, not talent,' I tell her with my eyes still glued to the TV.

'Don't watch it then Vinny, you whinger,' Sofia snorts. I can see she'd like to poke or kick me, but she knows she'll get told off if she does.

'Look Mum, your favourite act is coming on,' I inform her helpfully.

'Yes, "the grannies' choice",' Dad jokes. Mum flashes us her best 'you're in trouble now' look on her way to the kitchen. 'Yep, everyone votes for the cute kid. Mum's favourite. How predictable,' I say, bored now and picking up a book instead.

'Well I'm a cute kid,' says Sofia. 'Does that mean if I went on I'd get all the votes and win? When can I go on, Dad? I can't wait to be rich and famous!' Dad has said before that he doesn't want us girls to be part of the 'X-Factor generation'.

'Instant fame and fortune is short-lived and ill-advised,' he says. 'No, you need to work hard and aim for the stars and you may end up reaching the sun.'

'I will be a star – a genuine A-list celebrity though I don't really want to go on a TV talent show; there's far too much queuing up for auditions and the editing can make you look silly.' Sofia has an answer for everything. But Sofia hates waiting or working for anything; she's one of the 'I-want-it-now' generation my Dad complains about.

'Dinner's ready,' calls Mum and, for once, she brings it through to the living room and we are allowed to eat on a tray in front of the telly. Everyone who comes round gets full-on catering. No one leaves our house hungry, no one needs a formal invitation and good food is always on the menu.

Because my Dad was so poor when he was young we're not allowed to waste food. When Sofia tries to leave the food she hates it when he says, 'What about all those starving people in India?'

'Send it to them then!' she always replies sulkily. I think she's lucky she doesn't get a clout round the ear.

'You girls just don't know how lucky you are, you never go to bed hungry,' Dad says, repeating himself for the millionth time as we enjoy our feast while staring at the telly. 'When I was a boy, most nights we were hungry.' I turn to look at him. Whenever Dad thinks back to his childhood he has tears in his eyes.

'Were you really that poor, Dad?' I ask with sympathy.

'Yes, we were, but I was happy.' Dad smiles. 'I just become very sad when I see all we waste when so much of the world has so little.' I don't like everything Mum has put on my tray, but force myself to finish it. I feel bad after what Dad has said.

Britain's Got Talent finishes and I turn my attention to what the Aunties are talking about. The TV is a bit too loud to hear what's going on, but Sofia doesn't mind turning it off for the chance to hear the latest gossip. I roll my eyes now I can hear and realise they're still talking about weddings. The only matchmaking story I never get tired of is the one about how Mum and Dad met. I interrupt the Aunties and turn to Mum and Dad to ask them to tell the story again of how they met.

'Well,' says Mum, looking pleased I asked, 'I had enrolled at the college Dad used to run in India and I was one of his students.'

'It was all above board, nothing naughty going on,' he interrupts.

'We'd known each other a while when eventually we started dating, after I hounded your Dad for months. I pretended I needed extra help with my college work and one afternoon your Dad finally agreed to take me out for ice-cream and then that was it, he was hooked, we started dating. I used to make him little snacks with love notes in.' Mum giggles and looks at Dad. 'All the girls loved his poetry classes, especially when he used to read out his own poems. He wrote in Hindi, Urdu and sometimes English. The other girls thought he wrote his verses for them, but I knew he wrote his poems just for me. Even after we got married some of the students still gave him gifts, small things like handkerchiefs or sweets, with silly little notes. He brought them all home to me, you remember?' Mum says turning to Dad. Hang on, I haven't heard this bit of the story before!

'Yes, I remember everything.' Dad looks down at his hands, hiding a smile.

'If we fancied the Head of our school and sent him love notes Dad would kill us, so why was Mum allowed to?' Sofia splutters. 'I thought dating and all that stuff was much stricter back in India.'

'Ah,' says Dad, 'things were different then. It was all very innocent and with chaperones.' Dad looks like he's about to get up and leave the room but Sofia doesn't want the story to end.

'Hey, tell us the rest. What about my favourite bit where you ride into Mum's village and sweep her away on a beautiful white horse?'

'Ah, a wonderful match,' interrupts Aunty Jessie. 'I couldn't have done better for you myself,' she admits, sighing heavily.

Mum continues the story. 'Yes, his horse was white as snow and covered in garlands of pink, red and white flowers. Your Dad looked like a King. He wore a cream silk suit and hundreds of his friends and students lined the road up to my parents' house. I was waiting outside on our wedding day and when he reached where I stood, he lifted me up onto his horse and we rode away to our honeymoon. It was better than any Bollywood scene. In that village people still talk about our wedding.' Dad looks lovingly at Mum as she describes this. She blushes which makes her seem even more beautiful.

'That will happen to me one day. Just wait and see! I had five boyfriends all at the same time when I was five remember?' boasts Sofia. 'I liked Tony Lee the best.'

Dad always roars with laughter when Sofia talks about her "boyfriends", and she creates more and more to make him happy. Their friends – our aunties and uncles – are always curious to hear how many boyfriends she can conjure up and she tells some whopping fibs to keep them all entertained.

'She's in such a hurry to grow up,' Aunty Jessie pipes in. 'I will have to start looking for a nice boy for her very soon!' She laughs and winks at Mum.

'I don't think so, Jessie, it's entirely up to the girls when the time is right.'

Before Sofia can ask Aunty Jessie which boys she would match her with, Aunty Jessie turns her attention to me, squeezing my cheek hard. 'And Vinny, will Vinny go to college or shall we start looking for a nice boy now?' I flush red with anger and recall the taxi driver who was going to stop his daughter going to school by marrying her off to a cousin. I was going to college and nobody would ever stop me.

'No one is forcing me to marry, not ever,' I snap.

'Who said anything about forcing, I'm talking about a love match,' says Aunty Jessie with a reassuring pat.

'How can it be a "love match" if you do the choosing?' I demand.

'Why are you so upset?' Dad looks at me in surprise. I can see him wondering why his normally easy-going daughter is scowling and being so rude.

'I am not getting married,' I say firmly, feeling close to tears. Aunty Jessie's timing is pretty bad, touting for matchmaking business tonight was not going to work with me. Fortunately, she relents for now and the conversation turns back to Sasha and how successful that match is. When they have exhausted that conversation for the evening, the Aunties at last heave themselves up from the sofa. Mum and Dad go to see them off.

Sofia looks at me carefully.

'Your time to get married will come first I suppose. Who will you marry and do you reckon Dad would change his mind about letting us choose if we came home with a boy he didn't like?'

'I dunno, Sofia. I'm only fifteen remember. I don't want to talk about it. Leave it will you?'

'What's wrong Vinny? They won't really marry you off will they?' I'm saved from answering by Mum and Dad coming back into the room. There are some things Sofia just doesn't get yet.

'Come on madam, bedtime,' says Mum, pulling Sofia up off the sofa.

7

'Sit,' Dad says once Mum has taken Sofia to bed. He gently pushes me to the sofa before disappearing into the kitchen to put the kettle on. I lean back and pick at my fingernails.

A few minutes later he returns with mugs of hot chocolate for us both. 'Come on, out with it, what's wrong?' he asks, settling himself next to me.

'It's Aunty Jessie, she thinks she can decide how we live our lives, she thinks that the only thing girls dream about is getting married. But for girls like Tara and that... that taxi driver's daughters it's no dream, it's a total nightmare. I hate all this marriage stuff...' I mumble into my mug.

'The taxi driver's daughters?' Dad doesn't understand.

'The guy who drove us home from Sasha's wedding, what he said about his daughters, he's just a total monster!' I try to explain calmly but the words tumble out and I can feel tears of exasperation well up in my eyes. 'He's a total control freak. What gives him the right to decide who his daughters marry? He's living in the dark ages.'

'Oh, him.' Dad at last understands. 'I am afraid he might sound as though he's living in the dark ages but many people still share his views,' Dad explains softly.

'But you're not going to force me to marry, are you?' I ask, staring desperately into Dad's eyes.

'Force you? No! Never. Of course not,' Dad reassures me and wraps his arm around my hunched shoulders. 'Come on Vinny, cheer up. Don't worry about your Aunty Jessie going on about weddings tonight. You know what she's like, she even tried to sign next-door-aunty up to her silly matchmaking, and next-door-aunty is seventy-five!' I let out a weak chuckle and smile up at Dad, but I am a long way from feeling okay about it all and the smile soon disappears from my face.

'It's not just that, Dad, or even the taxi driver really. Tara from school still hasn't come back. I told you about her, remember? She supposedly went on holiday last year and she's never been seen or heard from since. She's still in India I guess, I think… I've been wondering about her, what if she's been forced to marry, she was only fourteen when she left! I didn't know her very well but I know she was like me, just a normal girl who wanted to go to school and have fun.'

Dad is frowning heavily now. 'Hey,' he says, 'come on, cheer up. What's happened to Tara is not acceptable but there is nothing you and I can do. We don't know her or her family. The police will be doing something about it I'm sure. Anyway, none of this will happen to you, you will keep going to school and we will always try to make your life as fun as it can be. Don't we have fun?' He tickles me as he says this. 'Let's have no more of this talk tonight. It's time for sleep and sweet dreams.'

8

Dad is always making new friends. He invites all sorts of people over to the house for dinner and it's great because they come from all over the world. Often their English isn't very good and Dad helps them fill in forms and stuff. He's generous like that.

It's the following Friday night when Dad and I pop to the shops for some milk and, I hope, a treat. Sofia stays home with Mum but she later wishes she'd come with us because we bump into the new family Aunty Jessie mentioned – the Kambis. They've moved into Holly Bush Gardens and Dad of course immediately invites them to the flat tomorrow night. Holly Bush Gardens is a bit grotty and not modern like the white flats we live in. It's all red brick Victorian and the flats are really tiny. Mum and Dad used to live there before Sofia was born. Later, when I mention the new family she says something that really shocks me.

'All the net curtains there are a funny greyish brown colour,' she tuts. 'Dirty beasts, they don't even wash them. And they cook everything in this really strong, stinky fish oil. The smell gets everywhere – in their clothes, their hair and it's always on their breath. Before you see them you can smell them a mile off.' I am so surprised to hear her be so mean and racist, that I just keep quiet.

Sofia demands to know everything about the Kambis.

'I met Abby,' I explain, 'and she's the same age as me. I think she's going to my school so I'll be able to help her settle in. Dad's invited them all around for dinner tomorrow night so you'll get to meet her little sister – I think she's about your age too.'

'I hope that's okay, Jasmine,' Dad quickly adds, putting an arm around Mum.

'Of course. I expect it from you to invite the whole neighbourhood to eat with us,' she says laughing.

The next morning, hours in advance, Mum starts preparing the evening's feast she has planned. The Kambis have four kids at home but they're only bringing three to dinner. They're coming for form filling and food.

'I'll help you, Mum,' I say, joining her in the kitchen.

'Me too, what can I do?' Sofia calls out.

'Well, tidy your room first, then you can help peel some potatoes,' Mum calls back.

'Oh that's not fair, I want to do the real cooking not the boring bits,' Sofia moans. 'Plus I'm in training. I've decided I'm going to be a celebrity chef, so I need lots of practice.'

'Well, that's nice, dear,' Mum says sarcastically. I think it's the tenth career Sofia's dreamt up that week.

Sofia quickly tidies her side of our room – or, I suspect, throws some stuff under her bed – then returns in full TV chef mode.

'Now, when peeling potatoes it's important to use a good quality peeler and to get the potatoes really wet. Dip them in a bowl of water first, yes that's right,' she says, holding up a dripping wet potato to the imaginary film crew. Mum and I roll our eyes. 'Now, if my assistant Vinny would like to demonstrate how to chop this lovely specimen. That's it, cut the potato in half, careful of the sharp blade, now place the flat end on the chopping board and cut it in small slices then across. Yes, well done.'

I sigh. 'Another twenty to go. You're not really going to talk through each one are you, Sis? Or I may have to chuck this bowl of potato peelings over your head.'

'Now dear audience, while the chore of cutting onions, potatoes and spinach - yes I know, bogey spinach - is under way, you can get on with the fun bit. Now you see how lovely this mixture is, it's umm… Mum, what's in it?'

'Gram flour, salt, red chilli powder, cumin seed and water.' Mum is mixing the batter ingredients for the pakoras.

'Yes, mix it so there are no lumps. Yes, very well done. Now we add the diced onions, potatoes and spinach – oh look we forgot the coriander – and mix together in a lovely metal mixing bowl like this one. Now the oil is very hot so take care. Now watch as Mum drops in one, two, three… five, yes, eight pakoras. Now we have to get a big flat plate. Line it with some kitchen paper to soak up the excess oil. Turn once, golden brown, get the ketchup on standby, yum, there you have it perfect potatoes and onion and spinach pakoras, super. Good job team, it's a wrap. That's what they say on TV.' She smiles at us, expecting applause. Of course there's none from us, her 'ungrateful family'. Instead I throw a tea towel at her and Mum just shakes her head.

The Kambis arrive at last and we are all introduced. Mr and Mrs Kambi are dressed very traditionally. Mrs Kambi is quite young, perhaps as young as Mum, although her face is lined and she looks tired. She has large brown eyes, but they are sad-looking with dark black circles under them, as if she hasn't slept properly for weeks. She is small and thin, dressed in a headscarf and long black coat. Mrs Kambi will get very hot if she keeps her coat on while she's in our flat.

Mr Kambi is wearing a boring grey suit and grey tie. I'm not sure why he is so dressed up to come and sit in our living room. His teeth are so white I think they'd shine in the dark. He looks a bit stern and serious though. The oldest daughter, Abby, is wearing a pretty headscarf. She's fifteen like me. Then there is her sister, Pinkie, who's a little older than Sofia and they've also brought a tiny baby boy called Abe who seems to do nothing but sleep. Pinkie hides behind Abby.

Mum's great feast is ready. We sit together quietly sharing our meal then Mum tells us to take Abby and Pinkie to our room to play with our toys.

'Go on, darlings, show them some of your things. I'm sure you've got lots to talk about,' Mum says.

'Shall we play Monopoly?' Sofia asks hopefully as the four of us hover in our small bedroom, not quite knowing what to do.

'Umm, yes,' Abby says sounding uncertain.

'Please let's not play that,' I say. 'Sofia's an awful cheat and it always ends in tears.'

'It's because you never win, Vinny,' Sofia serves back. 'Abby wants to play, don't you, Abby?' she says, dragging Abby over to our bed.

'No, we're not playing Monopoly and that's that,' I say firmly.

'Please,' she says with a great big smile plastered on her face as she pulls the Monopoly box out. I notice Abby and Pinkie pretend to look at something else. I glare at Sofia.

'Well, what else shall we do then?' she says, folding her arms crossly. Abby, Pinkie and I sit on the side of the bed and start to chat, just about what the schools are like and what movies they've seen. They seem happy to just chat but Sofia is intent on playing a game. I see her consider getting out my old doctor's kit and shake my head firmly. Sometimes I'm happy to be her patient, but today it seems a bit childish. She guesses I'm trying to impress Abby and so tries it herself.

'So Abby, what's your boyfriend like?' she asks cheerfully. Abby goes as red as a letterbox.

'Do stop it,' I whisper to her.

'What? Abby is fifteen so she must have had tons of boyfriends by now.'

'No, we're not allowed,' Abby says.

'Not allowed,' Sofia repeats. 'Why not?'

'My dad doesn't approve of girls dating and going out,' Abby explains in a hushed voice.

'Well when I was little I had at least ten boyfriends,' Sofia lies. Abby looks down and laughs, putting her hand over her mouth. Pinkie is so surprised her eyes are popping out of her head.

'There was, umm let me remember.' Sofia starts counting and muttering boys' names under her breath. '...and there was Tony-Lee, I still quite fancy him.'

'My dad would kill you if you were his daughter,' Pinkie declares.

'Oh yeah! Don't think so.' Sofia says defiantly although I'm quite shocked Pinkie would even think this.

Abby shrugs. 'Our family is very traditional, we're not allowed out at all except to see family. I was surprised we were allowed here when we don't really know your family yet, I guess it's because you don't have any brothers.'

'Why would that make any difference?' Sofia asks. She can be so naïve sometimes.

'Dad just doesn't want us to mix with boys. He says it's wrong, it would bring shame and disgrace to the family,' Abby explains, talking so quietly I can hardly hear her.

'I don't have a boyfriend either and I don't want one,' I admit shyly. I've never said that out loud to any of my friends. 'So just how strict is your dad?'

'He won't let us do anything at all, I'm not allowed to go to science club or anything after school,' Abby replies.

'Why?' I ask. 'What does he think you'll do?'

'He thinks I'll meet a boy. Besides, he says it's a waste of time for a girl to learn or study when all she needs to know is how to take care of her family,' Abby says, looking defeated.

Even Sofia seems to realise that what Abby's saying is really sad and I can see her trying to think of something to say to help her feel better.

'Well, boys are really boring you know. They pull your hair and kick footballs at you in the playground. You're not missing much,' Sofia says, truthfully for once.

Mum comes in at that point with a tray of Ribena and the baby crawls behind her.

'Here you go girls,' she says giving Sofia the smallest glass, because next-door-aunty told Mum Ribena made Sofia even more hyperactive. 'Your room looks nice, girls.' I've put up my favourite pop poster and Sofia has stuck up cuttings of the iPad and mobile she wants. 'Is it all right if the baby stays with you? He might like to play with that teddy,' Mum adds as she heads back to the living room.

'Your mum is super cool,' says Abby as soon as Mum's out of ear shot. Mum is wearing a pair of blue jeans and a simple T-shirt and with her hair tied back in a ponytail, she does seem pretty trendy.

Abe crawls over to Sofia who, as usual, is demanding attention being as she's the noisiest in the room.

'Let me show you my first aid skills,' she declares.

'Not on me,' I say.

She takes out the doctor's kit. I've had it since I was five. Sofia loves playing with it, more so after next-door-aunty gave her some extra bandages for it.

'Attention everyone. Let me show you how to do a head bandage,' she says. 'Who's going to be the patient?' Abe gurgles so Sofia takes that as consent. The baby doesn't seem to object, but probably only because he can't talk yet. Even Abby and Pinkie seem willing to join in now. Anything to avoid further awkward conversations about boys I imagine.

By now the baby looks like an Egyptian Mummy. We all laugh, including Abby, though she laughs the quietest and I wonder if it's because she thinks their dad will come in and tell them off. No sooner have I thought this than Abby suddenly suggests they leave. Sofia is being really loud now.

'We're being too noisy, Dad won't like it,' she says, biting her lip. Pinkie nods in agreement.

'Our mum and dad are very strict, not modern like yours. We might get in trouble.' Abby tries to shush Sofia but she defiantly starts to sing at the top of her voice just to show she won't be shushed. She then dances off into the living room as if to prove a point which I don't think is very kind of her. Abby unbandages Abe and picks him up so that the rest of us can reluctantly follow Sofia.

Sofia has gone quiet now and is sitting cross-legged on the floor near the plate of sweets the adults have been enjoying. Pinkie obviously thinks this is a good idea and joins her.

Mum is chatting to Mrs Kambi.

'Your life would be so much easier if you could learn some

English,' I hear her gently urge Mrs Kambi. 'It would be wonderful. You could help the children more with school and it would give you so much more independence. I could go with you to enrol for English speaking lessons, if you like?' Mum offers. But Mrs Kambi just shakes her head and looks nervously at her lap.

Our dads are still filling in forms and there doesn't seem to be any sign of movement so Abby , who has given her brother back to her Mum, and I head back to the bedroom. I can see Sofia torn between missing out on the teenager secrets we might share and the sweets under her nose that any moment she hopes she'll be offered.

I glance at Mr Kambi to see what he makes of all of us. He must find us really modern next to his family. He seems uncomfortable, especially with Mum.

I pick up Mum's make-up sales pack and offer some samples to Abby. She puts her finger in the lip gloss and applies some, summoning the courage to admire herself in the mirror. She smiles briefly at her reflection before wiping the lip gloss off.

'I'd better take it off, Dad won't like it,' she explains.

'Is your Dad really so strict that you couldn't have a boyfriend, if you wanted to, I mean?' I guess I know the answer already, but before Abby can respond Sofia bursts back into the room and Mrs Kambi calls for Abby to say they are leaving.

As soon as the front door closes Sofia asks what I thought of the Kambis.

'I like them, they're sweet,' I say honestly, 'and I think Abby is going to be in my class.'

'I'm not sure about Pinkie,' Sofia says with a pout, 'she was being too chummy with you. What were you and Abby talking about when we were gone?'

'Nothing really.'

'Please tell me, I promise I won't say anything. I bet they were dead good secrets.'

'There's nothing to tell,' I say forcefully and leave the room. I feel as though a new door has opened with a glimpse of another very different world. I want to know more about it and I think I'll get plenty of time to do that as I'm sure I have made a new friend in Abby.

9

On Monday morning at school Miss Metcalf comes in with a new girl. As I'd hoped, it is Abby. And it isn't just me who is excited. A new student in school always creates a buzz. Everyone hopes they'll be cool and interesting and not too nerdy. Abby looks understandably scared and won't look at anyone until I wave at her and she realises it's me.

'Vinny, Abby is in most of your classes. You'll show her round please, and make her feel welcome?' Miss Metcalf asks.

'Of course Miss,' I nod. Brilliant, I think to myself.

Abby is very quiet as I walk her to our next class.

'I can't believe that we are in the same class, what a cool coincidence. Everyone is really friendly you know, you'll soon settle in.'

'Oh that's good,' Abby says shyly.

At break time my friends Minnie, Alex and Sheila crowd around and start to quiz a red-faced Abby. Minnie is the first to start hurling questions at her.

'So why did you leave your last school. Which school did you go to?'

'Do you have a boyfriend?' Sheila butts in.

'What mobile have you got?' Alex interrupts.

'Are you on Facebook?' Sheila says, showing Abby her Facebook page on her mobile. Abby takes a deep breath.

'My dad got a job in London. I went to Elizabeth High School in Thornton. No I don't have a boyfriend,' Abby says, turning the colour of beetroot. 'Erm, what was the next question? Oh yes,

I've just got an old Nokia.'

'It's not a Smartphone then?' Alex is not impressed.

'No, it's my dad's old one. And I don't use Facebook either,' Abby looks mortified. 'We don't have a computer at home.' Everyone suddenly looks sympathetic, assuming that Abby's family is really poor I expect. Minnie, the nominated girl in charge (nominated by herself that is), starts again.

'You'll love it here,' she says warmly, 'it's great fun and none of us bite, honest.'

'Hey, homework's a total drag whichever school you're at,' Alex chips in.

'Yes but we do have GCSEs next year,' Minnie reminds us.

'Shut up Minnie,' we all say and Abby lets herself smile a bit, clearly relieved that my friends haven't given up on her already.

'I'm going to science club after school,' I tell Abby as we all head to our next class. 'Can't you come please, it's great fun, we get to do some really cool experiments.'

'Not sure I'd be allowed,' Abby says in a very hushed voice. 'Remember what I said about my dad? Anyway, Mum will need me home to help with my younger sister and brothers, she's not been well lately.'

'The lesson is only for 45 minutes. Besides, I can walk home with you. Surely your Dad won't object, he knows my family and you only live around the corner from me?'

'Oh, okay,' Abby agrees, I probably shouldn't have pressured her but I like her a lot already. I feel she has the makings of a new best friend and I can see she wants me to like her too.

As we wait for science club to start we sit on high stools at the back of the lab whispering to each other. Having got to know my group of friends better, Abby's already much less shy about sharing stories about herself and we're all riveted. 'My dad thinks that girls don't need much schooling,' she admits. 'My older sister Anna was taken out of school really young. We haven't seen her since she went away to be married.'

'What do you mean, you haven't seen or heard from your sister?' I say in total disbelief.

'My parents tricked her, not that it was very difficult. Anna just didn't imagine they'd ever do anything like that. They told us we were going home to visit family but what we didn't know was that my dad had already arranged for her to get married while we were there.' We are stunned. Just then our teacher arrives, bringing Abby's story to an abrupt end. My mind races. The taxi driver was one thing, but I can't believe a forced marriage like this has occurred in a family I know.

Forty minutes later we're packing away our books. I'm desperate to ask Abby more questions but she's excitedly babbling away about the experiment we just tried out.

'That was so cool trying to make sparklers with those compounds, shame they weren't dry in time,' she says.

'Don't worry, Miss said we can light them next week,' I reassure her.

'Erm, I'm pretty sure my Dad won't let me come again. Anyway, I've got to run.' Abby bolts out the door before I can say anything more. I run to catch her up in the hallway, after all I did promise her we could walk home together.

'Hey wait, slow down,' I say, confused as to why she can't just hang on for me.

'I've got to get back home, sorry, look I'll see you at school tomorrow.' Abby waves over her shoulder and runs off down the street. I walk the rest of the way home slowly, thinking about what Abby has said. I have to find out more. I decide to call her after tea or I'll never be able to sleep without knowing the full story.

Mum and Sofia are already home and Dad comes in soon after. We have the usual chatty tea together, swapping stories about our day.

'I got 19 out of 20 for my spelling today,' Sofia says, beaming.

'That's great darling,' say Mum and Dad at the same time. I pat her on the head just as she scowls and bangs the table. 'But then it wasn't fair 'cos Miss deducted three marks for talking in the test.' All three of us can't help ourselves and we burst out laughing. Every day there's something Sofia declares as unfair.

'Okay, Miss It's-Not-Fair, help your sister clear the table. I have a nice pudding for you,' Mum says smiling.

After dinner is cleared away and Mum, Dad and Sofia collapse on the sofa to watch TV, I tell them I'm going to my room. Sofia jumps up and follows me into the bedroom. I don't want to let on that I'm trying to call Abby in private as then I'll never get rid of her.

'Ah Sofia, I need to be alone for a bit, okay?'

'It's not f...' she starts but before she can finish Dad calls her back to see something on TV.

'Let your sister be, darling; she's a teenager now and needs some space,' I hear him say and at that moment I'm so grateful my father's nothing like Abby's. I flop on to the bed and dial Abby's number. We swapped mobile numbers earlier in the day.

'Hi Abby, it's me Vinny, can you talk?'

'Hi, yes good timing, Dad has just gone to work and the kids are in bed already.'

'I've been thinking about what you said about your sister Anna,' I say, wasting no time on formalities. 'We got interrupted and I'd really like to find out what happened to her. How could she just be sent away like that without school noticing or something?'

'Dad made Anna drop out of school in year nine. A school welfare officer came round to check on her once and Dad just told them she was being home educated.' Abby's voice is so quiet, I guess she doesn't want to risk her mum overhearing her gossip about Anna. 'No one ever checked again and we've moved house a few times. Dad made Anna stay home and look after all of us. As she got older she was never allowed out, not even to get the shopping. Anna wasn't very good at school so at first she wasn't bothered about not going, but when she realised her life was going to be spent at home looking after the family

she got fed up. She was okay at helping Mum but she really struggled with the cooking. Anna was always burning things and she couldn't concentrate on anything for long. I found myself trying to help her with her chores to stop her being shouted at by Dad all the time.' Abby sounds really upset. I so want to do something to help her.

'That's really awful, your poor sister. There must be a way you can get in touch with her. We could think something up.'

'There isn't, Vinny. It's too risky. I really miss her you know, but I don't know how or when I will ever see her again.' I can hear Abby crying. Every secret she tells me seems to get worse and worse and I feel so helpless. And what if Abby is to be married off next? It seems unimaginable but she's already older than her sister was when she was taken out of school.

'I'm so glad I've got you to speak to,' Abby eventually manages to say, distracting me from my darker thoughts. We chat some more, me mainly trying to cheer her up with stories of my sister's latest ridiculous antics. Finally we say goodnight and we each go back to sit with our very different families.

10

Abby's family soon visit our flat again but her dad's busy working at the restaurant so he doesn't come. This time we're also introduced to Abby's cousin, Sarina. She's six months older than Abby and has a huge family. Their dads are brothers. Sarina shares a room with her sister in a big house in Bradford. Sarina is dressed in a long black burkha.

'Wow, why are you so covered up?' Sofia blurts out once we're in the privacy of our bedroom.

'Don't be so rude,' I say, feeling my face turn red with embarrassment. 'Oh it's okay, my parents insist that if I go out I have to be totally covered up,' Sarina says, removing her burkha and throwing it on the bed. We gasp. Underneath she's wearing a really cool blouse and skin-tight jeans. Her nails are painted bright red and her lipstick is the same shade. Sarina is so beautiful that Sofia and I can't stop staring at her. Talk about Bollywood potential; she has huge brown eyes and eyelashes so long she looks like she has false lashes on.

'Oh wow, no wonder you are all covered up,' I say, laughing.

'Wow!' Sofia echoes, 'Who knew that you'd be dressed like that underneath. Can I try it on?' she asks, pointing at the burkha.

'If you like.'

We all fall about in hysterics as my daft sister prances around in the tent-like burkha singing at the top of her voice.

Sarina's mobile beeps and she takes out a very cute looking Blackberry. Sofia's eyes light up. It beeps again.

'Let's have a look,' Sofia pleads, jumping up next to Sarina who's trying to read the messages.

'You're far too young, besides they're private,' Sarina says, laughing and holding her phone close to her chest.

'I need a mobile phone. It's not fair; Mum says I can't have one and that I have no one to call anyway, but that's not true. I could talk and text for hours, I know I could.' I suspect that's what Mum's worried about. 'When I was little I used the phone to talk to the speaking clock until Mum got huffy about the cost and made me stop. Aaah, it's not fair.' Sofia buries her face in the bed.

'I haven't been excluded or anything, but I've been off school for months now,' Sarina says coolly, looking at her nails.

'Stop it! You bunk off school and your mum and dad know, no way?' Sofia is impressed. Little does she know.

'Exams are for swots.' Abby and I exchange anxious glances. I know she must be thinking about Anna.

'I think exams are just there to test us,' Sofia says, remembering one of Dad's jokes. No one laughs but Sofia blathers on oblivious. 'So you stay off school and your mum and dad let you. That's too cool.'

'Well instead of being at school Sarina does have to look after all her brothers and sisters and help her mum cook and clean,' Abby says a bit sharply. 'Sarina used to go to school but her Dad thinks exams and schooling are wasted on girls as they only need to get married and keep house and look after the children and the elders, so what good can books do them?'

'Nothing, I guess,' Sofia says very matter-of-factly, agreeing without really understanding Abby's meaning.

'Can your mum and dad adopt me?' Sofia asks Sarina. I nudge Sofia and give her a 'stop it' look. 'Well Mum and Dad never stop nagging us to do school work, do they!' Sofia snaps at me. We sit in silence for a moment, then Sofia, who has been staring at Sarina's jeans for the past five minutes says, 'You must have sprayed them on.'

'Dad's got a factory, he makes all kinds of ladies' clothes,' Sarina informs us. 'He's making skinny jeans at the moment.'

Sarina's mum is a housewife and looks after the children. Their dad is very strict. He insists all his children respect him and that the girls dress very modestly, which I find odd when you think about what his factory makes.

'I got one of the guys at the factory to make and adjust these jeans just for me,' Sarina says dreamily.

'Your dad would kill you if he saw what you wore under that,' Abby says as she looks towards the burkha, which has been thrown in a heap on the bed.

'I live two lives; one where I'm the perfect obedient daughter that does everything my parents want, and the other where I dress and behave however I want,' Sarina giggles.

'So apart from daydreaming about this hunky skinny jean maker, do you fancy him?' Sofia asks cheekily. Abby looks shocked.

'No comment,' Sarina responds unblinkingly and starts texting again.

'Your boyfriend?' Sofia says trying to sneak a look at her mobile but Sarina slips it back into her pocket. 'So tell us about your double life. We're good at keeping secrets, aren't we Vinny.'

'There really isn't much to say,' she says and she quickly puts an end to Sofia's queries by offering to show us all how to do really clever cane row plaits. She does my hair first and I have to say it looks great.

'Me, me, me, my turn next,' Sofia begs. As Sarina combs Sofia's hair ready for plaiting, her face becomes more serious.

'I'm going to get married,' Sarina says quietly as she plaits. Oh no, not her too, I think. Nobody says anything. 'I am,' Sarina says, knowing we don't believe her.

'Mr Denim?' Sofia asks hopefully. I barely dare listen to the answer.

'No, of course not, it's someone Dad's chosen. It's all been organised for this August.'

'What about school?' I ask, not knowing what else to say. 'School's important, having an education you know, every girl needs one.'

'You are such a nerdy swot, Vinny,' scoffs Sofia.

We've finished plaiting now and so move on to Mum's Avon

kit. Sarina knows how to use make up properly and shows us how to use black eyeliner to make our eyes look bigger.

'Put some on me, Sarina,' Sofia demands. 'Go on, tell us more, Sarina.'

'It's true, I haven't been to school and I've also been stuck indoors for months,' she confides. Her confident tone seems to be wearing off quickly. 'Dad's really paranoid I'll run away. The only chance I get to go out of the house alone is if I sneak through the window and slide down the drainpipe, and that's now so loose it's almost falling off. I'm scared of what Dad'll do if he finds out. And apart from texting I don't even get to speak to anyone much as Dad only lets me have enough credit for essential calls, so I have to rely on friends to top up for me.' Sarina doesn't seem so super cool now; she looks scared and uncertain. Sensing the change in atmosphere, she braves a smile. 'Hey, I miss not being at school, but I don't miss the homework!'

'Yeah, it's not all bad, Sarina,' Sofia chips in, 'no exams, no revision.' Still smiling Sarina half-heartedly nods her head in agreement, but her beautiful eyes look so sad.

'Mostly I miss just having a laugh and being me when I'm away from home. Now I'm at home all the time, there's no escape from being "the good-daughter-soon-to-be-a-wife". The weirdest bit is that when I get married I won't live in Bradford anymore. I'll live abroad in my husband's family house with his parents, brothers and sisters, their wives and kids.' I glance at Abby to check her reaction but she's frowning and looking at her nails. I think she knew all this already and she probably also knows she won't be seeing Sarina again once she's gone. I feel for her as it must bring back awful memories of losing Anna. And she must also be thinking of her own future too. What a horrible thought.

'That must be one big lump of a house if you're all going to live there!' Sofia shrieks.

'I don't know; I haven't seen it,' says Sarina and even Sofia looks surprised for a brief moment before wailing, 'I bet it's awesome, a real Bollywood palace! It's not fair, I want to stay off

school and live in a big house too.' Oh Sofia, I think, you don't know what you're saying. What's not fair is that Sarina is being taken out of school at just sixteen years old to be sent away and married to someone she's never met and who she doesn't want to marry. I glance at Abby in horror but try to hide my feelings by smiling at Sarina in what I hope is a reassuring 'It'll be okay' sort of way. What else can I do?

11

Sofia is being so nosey, asking Sarina so many questions, it's embarrassing. Thankfully she hears Mum coming in the front door and she goes charging to meet her to peer in the shopping bags. Mum has been up to London to Oxford Street. Her timing is perfect, with Sofia out of the way I can ask some serious questions without her interrupting.

'Sarina has a picture on her phone of her secret friend,' Abby says.

'I will miss him,' Sarina says wistfully as she shows me a picture of her factory boyfriend.

'So you do have a boyfriend,' I exclaim incredulously. 'How do you manage that with your Dad being so strict? And you're still going to get married to a complete stranger?'

'Well, he's only sort of my boyfriend, and my Dad won't let me marry him,' Sarina lowers her voice to a whisper, 'because he's English, so I don't have much choice do I? Anyway, I'm not marrying a total stranger; he's a cousin, though I've never met him.' I just can't believe Sarina is so calm about it all. It's as if she's sleepwalking. Maybe she's in denial about it. It's all too much to take in. I feel myself get cross towards Sarina.

'How can you even think about doing this, getting married to a man you've never met?' I demand.

'I don't have a choice, do I?' Sarina mutters.

'Why don't you? Why don't you just ignore them, refuse to go?' Sarina's too upset to answer so Abby speaks up.

'I don't think you can understand, Vinny. It's different for you, your parents are really liberal in comparison to ours. If we disobeyed them, we'd be on our own. They wouldn't just be annoyed or ground us, they'd disown us, cast us out. We'd have nothing and we'd bring great disrespect on our whole family; it would impact our brothers and sisters too. We could never face any of them again.' Abby sounds sad rather than angry, which confuses me even more.

'But I thought… I thought in this day and age we must all have a choice,' I say, but quietly as I'm no longer sure of what I'm saying or know.

'Maybe when you get out there you can make your Dad change his mind,' I suggest to Sarina hopefully.

'Do you really think so?' Sarina looks happy for a moment but then shrugs. 'I'm not so sure, you don't know my Dad. Marriage and all that stuff, it's family business that the men decide on and nothing to do with us girls.'

Sofia comes back into the bedroom, demanding to know what we've been talking about, and looking annoyed that she's missed out on 'teenager' secrets again. For once I'm grateful for her interruption. Then Mrs Kambi calls Abby and Sarina to remind them they need to go soon; there's a big family get together planned for the evening. As Sarina puts her burkha back on it's as if she's become a different girl again.

Before they go Sofia asks Sarina to tell us a couple more rude jokes and she laughs so hard I worry she could wet herself.

'Please come over again before you go off and get married,' I whisper over her shoulder as we hug goodbye.

'We need to go to Brick Lane for wedding shopping,' Sarina says, 'so I will be back down soon, I promise.'

Goodbyes are said all round and then they're gone. I sit on the bed afterwards and try to understand Sarina's situation. Why couldn't Sarina try standing up to her parents and if she left them would it be so bad? If her parents disowned her, what would that mean? Would it mean she would never see or hear from them again? How could parents do that to their child? Loving parents is all I've ever known and I just can't imagine being in Sarina's shoes.

12

'Vinny come see what we've got for you,' Dad calls. It's a Saturday evening and Mum and Dad have been shopping on Oxford Street for the afternoon while I did some homework and Sofia played at next-door-aunty's. Mum and Dad have bought us some new skirts and T-shirts for the summer hols but surprisingly, for once they're not identical. I look at Mum and she instantly understands.

'You're getting older, you need different things from your sister.'

'Thanks, Mum.'

Dad has also bought Mum some really cool trousers and there was a Marks and Spencer's bag amongst their treasures so we knew he had something new too. Dad buys all his clothes from M&S. We try on our clothes and do a silly little fashion show.

As we change back into our old clothes I talk to Dad and Mum about Abby and Sarina's visit.

Sofia starts to talk about the wedding.

'Sarina isn't that excited about it, if anything she's a bit down about getting married. She won't have a lovely fluffy dress I guess 'cos I bet she'll wear a sari, with yards and yards of silk, and hundreds of gold sequins. She's marrying a cousin she's never met you know and she doesn't have to go to school anymore.' Sofia doesn't notice our parents' suddenly serious expressions. Dad says it's not good that Sarina has already missed so much school, but Sofia defends our newest friend.

'Her mum's got two sets of twins you know, so Sarina has to stay home to help her.'

'Sofia, you should know by now how important it is for everyone to have a good education.' Dad's tone is frustrated and even Sofia has the decency to notice this and to stop chattering on about dresses. 'If every girl across the world had the chance of an education it would lead to more freedom of choice and finally break the cycle of women and girls being impoverished.' Dad bangs the coffee table as he says this.

'It's not right, we all know that, but what can we do Dad; what can the police do, what can we do to stop this?' I say, grasping at the opportunity for some answers.

'It's very difficult, girls, it is an issue that this government is still grappling with, but the law has been changed now and forced marriage is now illegal.' If Sarina is being forced out of the country, there are things that can be done to help her Mum glances at Sofia who has gone very quiet and then claps her hands.

'Come on, enough of this for now. It's late, let's have some dinner and then you can get ready for bed. Early night for you both, though Vinny, you can stay up a little later.'

A little later, Sofia and I get ready for bed.

'I've been thinking about it and maybe bunking off school isn't worth it if you can't have any fun and have to act all grown up and do cleaning and stuff. What do you think, Vin?'

'Hmm?' I'm too wrapped up in my own thoughts to be able to answer her questions.

I'm not really taking in what Sofia is saying, because my head is pounding with hundreds of different thoughts about Sarina and Abby.

'Hadn't we better warn Sarina that she's about to become impoverished? That she won't have the same rights anymore like Dad said? We need to fire her up and tell her to go back to school and get some exams. So that if she wants to she can stand on her own two feet. How can she marry someone she doesn't love or has never seen? Hey, why are you so grumpy, why won't you answer?'

'Sorry Sofia, I don't feel up to talking.'

Sofia gives up but carries on talking to herself. 'Besides, it's boring staying home all day doing housework and looking after all those kids. Where's the fun in that? Vinny, what's eating you? Answer me.' She stamps her foot and flings the covers over herself.

Now in my pyjamas I quietly say 'Night' to Sofia and go back to the living room to watch more TV and enjoy my later bedtime. As I close the bedroom door I hear Sofia say, 'But it's just not fair.'

13

It's Monday lunchtime and I'm in the canteen clutching my lunch tray looking for Abby. She has a packed lunch every day as her parents worry about what she'll eat otherwise. It's a bit chilly so we huddle to eat on a table nearest to a radiator. Our school is old, Victorian to be exact, so the heating's not great and sometimes it's on in the summertime, though today we're glad of it.

I've been worrying about everything Sarina told us on Saturday and am desperate to hear what Abby thinks about it all.

An 'arranged marriage' is what Abby calls her cousin's wedding but 'arranged' is just a word to make it sound better. My friend Sasha's marriage was arranged; she was introduced to lots of different boys, but she never had to do it. She was given a choice of who she could marry. With Sarina it's different, they're forcing her to do it, they don't care how she feels about it and she's scared.

'I was surprised to hear about Sarina's wedding. I can't imagine her getting married so young and in such a traditional way. She's so young and she's a bit wild too isn't she?' I stopped talking, feeling embarrassed as if I've said too much. 'Anyway, I'm not interested in boys much yet, are you?'

'Sarina doesn't have any choice, that's why she makes it sound as though she doesn't mind. As for me and boys, huh you're kidding!' says Abby, sounding bolder and angrier than I've ever heard her. 'As if I'd be able to have a boyfriend even if I was interested. My Dad will know who I will marry before I do! '

'He really is strict isn't he. Are you worried about what will happen to you?'

'Oh yes, he rules our house. I'm never allowed out. I'm only allowed a mobile because Mum doesn't know how to use one and he always checks my texts and phone calls.

'He thinks I'm calling boys.' We both laugh, it seems so silly; the two of us are probably the only fifteen year old girls in our school, in London even, who actually don't want boyfriends.

I stop laughing and bite my lip. It's not funny really, any of it.

I don't know what to say really, so I tell her about Tara Tally, who'd disappeared into thin air. The police came in to interview all the girls in our year group but I couldn't help, I barely knew poor Tara. Nor did I really understand what was going on at the time but now I'm beginning to see how things might have been for Tara.

I look around for Tara's old school friends. I spot Aneeta and Sylvia just as they're standing up to leave the lunchroom. They're chatting away as if everything in their lives were normal. I wonder if they knew what was going to happen to Tara and if, like me, they did know but didn't have any idea what to do about it.

On Sunday afternoon the doorbell goes. I open the front door and am surprised to see Abby and Pinkie standing there without their mum or dad. They've come over to pick up some paperwork Dad has done for their parents. 'Hi girls, we're just about to have lunch, join us,' says Mum waving them in. 'Do you like pizza and garlic bread?'

'Umm…' Pinkie and Abby look a bit embarrassed.

'It's really nice,' Sofia enthuses, knowing the girls would like to stay but are too shy to say yes.

Dad calls out from the kitchen. 'Don't worry, I'll phone your father to say you are staying for lunch.'

'Come on girls, who wants to cut up some salad for me?' Mum asks as she heads to the kitchen. Pinkie rushes to join her, keen to help, while Abby flops down on the sofa next to me.

'Sofia, put your homework away now and give me a hand laying the table, please,' Mum says.

'All's fine with your dad. So how's school, Abby?' asks Dad as he hangs up the phone.

'It's really good, I love science,' Abby replies, smiling broadly.

'That's excellent, my dear. A good education is an absolute must, it will open up so many doors for you.' Dad is getting serious, as usual. I want to tell him that he doesn't need to tell Abby, he needs to tell her father, but I don't dare. But surprisingly, instead of just nodding like we always do, Abby actively agrees then says, 'I wish my Mum could speak English so she could understand what I do at school. I think it's awful for Mum, Dad makes all the decisions and does all the shopping. She just stays indoors all the time, except when she visits family, but normally she's too busy with cooking, cleaning and looking after all the kids.'

'Your mum has it pretty hard,' Mum agrees as she pops her head round the door and waves everyone into the kitchen.

As Dad slices the pizza and serves us, Abby whispers to me. 'I can't believe your dad does housework and cooks! My dad has never even been in our kitchen except to eat.'

Dad overhears her confession. 'I'm far too fond of eating not to cook,' he says, patting an imaginary huge fat tummy. We all laugh.

When we're finished, Abby and I head to the bedroom to listen to some music. Sofia goes to follow us.

'Not you madam, you still have homework to finish.' Sofia screws up her face at Mum and opens her mouth to wail, but before she can the three of us all chorus. 'It's not fair!' She stomps her feet angrily as she grabs her schoolbooks, but she has a smile on her face. To Sofia any attention is good.

'Pinkie, sit with me and have a biscuit while Sofia finishes her homework,' says Mum kindly allowing Abby and me to make our escape.

As soon as we are alone I ask about her cousin. 'Have you heard from Sarina?'

'No, we haven't and we probably won't. She doesn't have access to a computer and there won't be a phone that she can use. I know this sounds uncaring but, just as with Anna, I have to try and forget about Sarina.

'I'm sorry,' I say weakly.

'You know the same will happen to me...' Abby says this so quietly I'm hoping I didn't even hear her right. 'When the time comes,' she continues, 'I will have to go back home to marry some cousin whether I want to or not. I might never see my family again once I leave and as you know we haven't heard from Anna in two years. Why should I be any different?'

'No!' I want to make Abby stop saying these things, I want them not to be true. 'Please, not you too.' I admit I've pushed away thought of this whenever it occurred to me but it was easy as Abby never confirmed it. Now I was forced to face it. How could something like this happen to Abby?

'But why, why you too? Why is it so important to your mum and dad to do this?'

'It's about debts owed, about helping cousins and friends to come to this country. A lot of the sense of what is owed goes back many generations.'

At that point Sofia bounces into the room, she's finally finished her homework, but her timing is rubbish. Dad says it's time for Abby and Pinkie to go home. Sofia begins to protest and Dad takes pity on her.

'You can walk them home,' he offers, 'and don't forget to stop in the playground for half an hour on the way back.'

We walk as far as the park and wave the girls goodbye. I haven't been able to ask Abby anything more about what she said while Sofia and Pinkie were with us.

'What did you do in the bedroom?' Sofia asks once we're on the swings.

I shrug. 'Not much.'

'I bet you were telling secrets,' she whines.

I lie and tell Sofia she didn't miss anything, that there were no secrets, we'd just been chatting about school and friends, nothing more. I wish this were true.

15

I mooch around the house the rest of the day thinking about Abby and Sarina. My head is whirling with this new and scary world that I am learning more and more about.

I think nobody has noticed my mood but Dad must have seen that I am quiet and withdrawn. At about half seven he asks Mum to take Sofia to bed.

'It's not fair,' she complains as usual. 'Why can't I stay up?'

'Remember you have separate bedtimes now darling. You still need an early bedtime,' Mum explains patiently as they head to the bedroom.

'So, what is it that's troubling you now, my little angel?' Dad asks, patting the sofa space next to him. 'You've had a rumpled frown on your face all day.' He strokes my hair, but rather than soothing me, his gentle affection irritates me and sets me off on a rant.

'Why should any parent feel they have the right to decide whether or not their kids get married! Never mind deciding who they can marry. What gives them the right? Why can't girls just marry because they fall in love? Why should anyone have the right to force them?' I'm so furious but I can feel tears surging to my eyes. I'm desperate for Dad to make it all better, to give me all the answers and make the world all right again, as he always could when I was a little girl. He wraps his arms around me but it isn't enough. I push away.

'Sarina is getting married even though she doesn't want to,' I say, calmer now, 'and when Abby's dad decides the time is right, she'll also be forced to marry whoever he wants her to.'

When Dad finally speaks, it's with great empathy and softness.

'I understand your anger. I have seen this sort of thing many times in my life and each time I feel the same way. Some parents get all tied up in tradition and wanting to hold onto the values they grew up with, to raise their children the same way they were raised, but the world doesn't stand still. Their values don't necessarily work in this newer world and not everyone can deal with how our world has changed. What they also don't realise is that even back home a lot of people have moved on, their values have adapted. Your cousins in India are now allowed to date and choose who they marry.'

'But why can't Abby's parents see what they're doing isn't right?' I interrupt.

'Nearly all parents want what's best for their children even if sometimes they're wrong. Even your mum and I don't get everything right, though I hope you know we would never force you to do anything you didn't want to do.'

'Abby also told me that her big sister Anna was tricked into getting married,' I confide.

'What do you mean?' Dad asks, his eyebrows raised. He glances up at Mum as she comes back into the room and sits opposite him.

'I was talking to Abby and she told me that their parents lied to Anna. They told her she was going back home for a holiday and then they made her get married and Abby hasn't seen or spoken to her since. Abby doesn't even know exactly where Anna is. And then last week Abby told me that she heard her dad shouting at her mother that she has to make Abby work harder in order to teach her how to cook and clean so that she doesn't bring shame on them or else Abby will be beaten like her sister was. What's worse is that Sarina must know all this, she knows what to expect, and yet she is still going out there to get married.'

'Poor Sarina and Abby too, this is horrible. We hear about these things but to have it going on with people we know really well is a shock,' Mum says, her voice gravelly with concern.

Dad shakes his head. 'There's little anyone can do if Sarina is prepared to go ahead with this. If she were being forced it would be a different matter. But she's sixteen and going there knowingly. No one can interfere to help,' Dad says flatly.

'Maybe the poor girl doesn't really understand what she is letting herself in for,' Mum adds.

'But Abby does, Mum. and she'll need our help, there's no way she would agree to an arranged marriage.'

'If Abby finds herself in this situation we will step in and help,' says Dad reassuringly.

'What will you do Dad?'.

'Hopefully it won't come to that,' says Mum, and I can sense that she's trying to convince herself as much as she is me.

'Maybe things will seem clearer in the morning,' Dad suggests, giving me a hug goodnight.

As I head to the door I pause and turn back. 'I love you Mum, I love you Dad,' I say and with more meaning than I've ever felt before.

'Love you too angel,' they say in perfect unison.

16

Abby and I sit at her kitchen table revising for our science exam. To be honest, Abby doesn't need to, she's a natural at it and I think she just enjoys helping me.

We hear the front door bang. It's Abby's mum returning from the shops.

The younger ones run in ahead of Mrs Kambi, sticky sweets in their hands. Mrs Kambi smiles at me and then without warning turns to Abby and launches into a full-scale tirade. I'm so shocked and embarrassed I pretend to be engrossed in my practice papers. I can normally understand most of what Mrs Kambi says, but she's talking so fast and with such passion that I don't get a lot of it. It's obvious they're arguing and before long, I'm ushered out of the flat by a mortified Abby who just whispers that she's sorry and she'll explain later.

I'm almost home when Abby texts me: Where are you, I need to see you now.

My heart pounds as I call Abby on her mobile. I've only known her for a few months but I know her well enough to realise she doesn't send messages like that without good reason. The argument must have got out of hand.

'What's going on, what was all that about?'

'I won't be like her,' Abby sobs when she answers.
'What's wrong, tell me, where are you?' I demand.
'The park'.
As I near the park I can see Abby sitting on the swings, all

hunched up.

I run as fast as I can and hug Abby who is still crying, her eyes are red and her nose is running.

'What's happened?' I ask, though I'm scared what the answer will be, I've never seen anyone this distressed before. 'Talk to me, what's happened? Please Abby, please tell me. I'll try to help, we're friends.'

After what seems like an age Abby regains her composure.

'I can't be like this, I can't, I can't end up like my sister and Sarina.' Abby isn't making much sense. I sit on the swing next to her and hold her hand.

'I hate them,'

'Who, Anna and Sarina?' I say, confused.

'No, Mum and Dad. Vinny, you have no idea, it's not like this for you, your mum and dad are normal.'

'Well, normal? I don't know about that.' I try to crack a joke as Sofia would but my timing is all wrong. 'Sorry, look, erm, just tell me everything about the argument from the beginning.'

'She started off saying that I should have been finishing washing the dishes, that I'm always daydreaming with my head in a book.'

'But she seemed so angry,' I reason.

'She only got so cross because she knows my dad will be furious if he finds out. She gets frustrated that I don't do as they say all the time. She says I mustn't waste my time with this nonsense,' she gestures at my school bag still over my shoulder, 'but she doesn't understand why it's so important. I tried to explain about our exam…'

When they fought, Abby, her face flushed with anger and embarrassment, had looked at me pleadingly, even though she knew I couldn't understand what they were saying. Now I realise she was willing me to back her up.

'Mum told me there's no point in studying because it's not important for a girl. That I should learn to cook properly and be quick at cleaning so I can keep my future husband and his family happy. It's all my mother ever learned and she knows Anna has suffered because she was always so slow. She doesn't want me to bring the same shame on her too. She doesn't want me to be seen as "another lazy Western daughter". All she cares about is how they appear to people who live hundreds of miles away.'

Abby told me once that her mum never mentions Anna so both Abby and I were surprised.

'Did you tell her you miss Anna, maybe that'll help her to realise that she shouldn't do the same to you?'

'Yes, and I asked her why Anna never writes to us, but she just said it's because Anna has a new family and she belongs to them now so she doesn't need us anymore. That's when she really lost it and I had to ask you to leave.'

I nod, trying to look like I understand, but I don't really. 'Did she say anything else after I left?'

'Only that the same had happened to her when she was even younger than me and that she never again saw her sister or mamma before they died.' We both sit in stunned silence. I can't imagine never seeing my family again, even though Sofia drives me mad sometimes. Unfortunately for Abby, she's already living with the reality of never seeing Anna again. Abby sighs when she sees the disapproval I'm unable to hide on my face.

'My father's a good man really,' she says weakly. 'Apparently he sent money after my mum's sister died to help her family.' I look at her confused. 'I still know it's not okay. I told Mum that too. I didn't even get to say goodbye to her. Why didn't she tell us Anna wasn't coming back?' Abby breaks down and covers her face with her hands, trying to hide her tears. I stroke her back and look up to see if anyone is about. The park is surprisingly quiet, there's just a few younger kids playing on the roundabout and a couple of boys kicking around a football. Anna takes a deep breath before continuing.

'I don't want to end up like Anna or my mum. I couldn't bear to leave my family.'

'Did you tell your mum that?'

'Of course, but she just looked away from me and tried to tell me what a handsome boy Anna's husband is, that Uncle Mohammed Jan chose well and I should be glad to have such a fine husband one day soon. You know I want to be a teacher, well, when I explained this to Mum, that I am top in my class and should be able to go to university, she said it was nonsense and I should put it out of my head immediately because even if she wanted me to study, my father would never allow it. I thought maybe she was softening but then she said going to college would "put more selfish Western ideas" into my head.'

'You're doing the right thing, keep fighting it. They've not done anything yet so you might be able to make a difference.' I know I'm clutching at straws but I feel it's the only way I can help. Before I've even finished though Abby is crying again.

'You don't understand...' she explains between sobs that come thick and heavy now, '...It's already started... She lost her temper...I told her she was always so tired, that she treats me like a slave...Then, she told me my dad is planning things with another family now. He's already picked a boy for me to marry soon...' I'm beyond shocked and stare at Abby whose pale face has never looked so desperate.

17

'I've got to get out of there, I've got to get away,' Abby's voice was sounding panicked now. But where will I go? You've got to help me, please!' I'm speechless but I squeeze her hand to encourage her to keep talking. 'They want me to be someone I'm not, Mum wants me to have the same life she has, being tied to the house. Vinny, she doesn't leave the house unless it's to go to the shops. I'm not like her, I'm not an obedient little girl from a village. I've grown up in England; I have an education. They've allowed me to see the possibilities in life and now I want to make my own choices but they want to take that away. I want more out of life than marrying a guy I don't know and don't love when I'm just fifteen. Look at me, this is the first time I've been to the park on my own in my whole life. My mum doesn't do anything, she has no life, no views of her own, it's all what Dad says, she's a bloody puppet.' I've never seen Abby so angry or heard her swear before; it's like now she's started there's no stopping her.

'And what about Anna! It's as if she never existed, what if something's happened to her? I would do anything to see her again, to make sure she's okay. I used to help her with her school work, and the housework. I worry so much about her. She was always so slow at everything; Dad hit her sometimes and Mum never stopped telling her off, so there's no way she'd cope without me there to help her. And since she's been gone I've had to do everything. Mum is always so exhausted; it's like she's given up on life. When I get home from school I have to cook the dinner, wash up, help Pinkie and my brother with their homework, do mine, get everyone to bed, then when Dad gets home at around eleven from the restaurant I have to serve him his dinner, clear away and then iron the uniforms, pack the school bags and make the packed lunches before I go to bed. Vinny, most parents nag their kids to study. I'm not even allowed to let my Dad see me doing homework.' Abby finally stops to take a breath.

'I had no idea it was so bad Abby, I'm so sorry. I can't believe what you've been going through alone, it's awful. How can you cope living like that?'

'I can't cope, that's the point... You're so lucky, your mum and dad, they support you, they love you as you are.' Abby says meaningfully.

'I really do have an easy life, don't I.' I'm humbled by everything Abby has said. 'I always thought Mum and Dad were a bit strict, always going on about homework and studying, but I can't imagine them saying there's no point to it all because I'm just a girl, that it's a waste for me to study.' I shake my head.

'It's not fair,' Abby says, and never have I heard it said with such truth. 'Why can't I just be a normal teenager and concentrate on school and having fun like you?' Abby asks. I have no answer. She's stopped sobbing and angrily pushes herself back and forwards, the chains of the swing making a snapping sound as she urges it higher and faster.

'I wish I could just fly away, just get out of here,' Abby says and I can see that she's half-thinking that if she goes high enough she just might take off. Her angry outburst is gone as fast as it came and she stops swinging and sags like an empty balloon. 'But I know I can't. What about Pinkie, what about the younger ones, who would look after them? Mum couldn't cope. I'm trapped Vinny, I really am.'

There's nothing I can say that will help and Abby knows this because she quietly says, 'I'd better go; I need to think about what to do.' We hug tightly then I look into her eyes.

'Let's both think about what to do,' I say. 'Will you be okay until we can figure something out?' She nods unconvincingly.

'Bye Abby, text me to let me know you got home okay and call whenever you need to.'

Abby walked back into their flat, her head hanging, concealing her expression of quiet determination.

'Where have you been?' Pinkie wailed, running over to give Abby a hug. Pinkie's hands were still dripping wet from washing up but it didn't matter. When Abby spoke she was quiet but strong.

'I'm sorry Mamma but I will not be married off and live the life you've led. I want more, I want to use my brain and marry if and when I'm ready.'

Her mother remained firm. 'You have no idea how lucky you are. You have so much freedom, you go to school, you have friends, you watch TV, you wear Western clothes.' Abby touched her blue headscarf and looked down at her loose black trousers and long grey jumper, all bought for her and intended to hide her body.

'But Mamma…' she began.

'Let's not talk about it again,' Abby's mum said softly, 'Besides the children are hungry.'

'I will never, ever end up like you,' Abby said in English under her breath. 'I don't know how yet but I will make my life different.'

18

It's the last day of term before the summer holidays and I'm almost skipping as I make my way to school. I see Abby walking with Minnie a little way ahead and I break into a run.

'Abby, hey summer hols! I can't wait. And you, you lucky thing, you're off to Heathrow tonight aren't you?' I hear Minnie say as I catch up with them. 'Are you looking forward to the wedding?'

'Mmm, yeah,' Abby mumbles in reply but Minnie has already run ahead to catch up with Alex.

'It will be so great to see Anna and I hope she can come, and sorry to be so negative, Vinny, but to be honest the rest of it will be a bit painful.'

'Why?' I ask, feeling a little stupid for needing to.

'We will be bossed around all day of course and we'll have to do all the housework and help with the cooking and the boys – and you can guarantee they'll all be spoilt and horrid because boys are always favoured. They'll get to play out in the garden or climb the mango trees while we're treated like slaves; it's hardly fair.'

'Oh, I see.' I did see too, because the one boy we had met from her family apart from the baby was Addi her brother and he was a spoilt little brat. He never had to do any chores and loved to give orders to the girls and even his mum.

'And Dad's brother,' she rolls her eyes, 'is even stricter, if you can believe that.' With that we turn in to the school gate to begin our last day of year ten.

After a day filled with not very much but chatting, tidying up and watching a movie, I said goodbye to the gang with a special hug for Abby.

'I hope you enjoy it a little, Abby, it's our last holiday before school gets serious, and at least it will definitely be warm and sunny, unlike here hey! And take care, yes?' She nodded as she returned my crushing hug and then turned and waved again before she walked away.

I didn't know it then but it would be a long time before I saw Abby again.

19

'It's stupid, I hate teachers; they spoil everything. It's the summer holidays, so it should be just six weeks of just lying in bed, watching TV, messing with Vinny, eating ice cream and having fun. Instead they've given us lots of homework. Whoever heard of doing homework in the holidays!' Sofia moaned to next-door-aunty as she banged her bag onto the table. She was there for tea as she only had a half day of school on the last day of term.

'My teacher said I don't take school seriously enough – she ganged up with my year six teacher and they want me to write a diary over the summer holidays. What a bloody cheek!'

'Any more of that language and you'll have to wash your mouth out with soap and water, madam,' scolded next-door-aunty.

Next-door-aunty usually let Sofia off with worse behaviour than this but today she was taking her babysitting role seriously.

'Sorry,' Sofia said meekly. 'But it's not fair, really it's not, why should I waste my holiday writing a diary? Besides, Dad told us diaries are private so I won't let them read it. I'll get a book that locks and say, "Oh sorry Miss Nosey Parker, I have done a diary and written a hundred words a day but it's private, you can't read it".'

Next-door-aunty smiled and tickled Sofia under the chin. 'You are such a little horror you really are, don't you let your dad hear you talking like that, he'll have your guts for garters, he really will. You are a right madam sometimes.'

'Me? Vinny's the madam, she's going to tell Mum and Dad that I have to do it. And Dad'll insist on checking it every night.'

Before long, Sofia was happily eating next-door-aunty's chips and she forgot all about school. When she heard her parents on the stairs she leapt up, kissed next-door-aunty goodbye, grabbed her bag and clattered back to the flat for dinner – her second of the night.

The next night is the first proper day of the holiday and 'Drats,' complains Sofia, Dad hasn't forgotten about the diary. 'Come on everyone, listen to Sofia,' Dad insists. We are all sitting in the living room after dinner. Dad insists we turn the telly off in the evening for at least an hour of 'family time' because he thinks we've been watching TV all day, which we have of course.

Sofia pretends to read it out. I quickly realise what she's doing but Mum and Dad are listening carefully.

'Dear Diary, my only true friend, I am so all alone, with just the TV for company,' she says with false sincerity. 'Yes, dear Diary, I am very, very sad. I've been locked up in our flat all day while my parents were out at work.' She stops. Mum looks horrified.

'Show me that,' she says, taking the diary from Sofia.

'It could be private,' Sofia says, teasingly.

'Aah, she's only mucking about. Come on darling, read what you've written properly,' she says, sounding relieved.

'Dear Diary. Day one of the Summer Holidays. Well the sun shone for exactly thirty-five minutes, so no "summer" in the holiday yet. Had Monster Munch for breakfast. Watched some TV. Dad came home for lunch and brought some chips. Vinny promised to set me up a Facebook account when I am old enough so I'll tell you all about that then. Signing off till then. And then I put three kisses,' Sofia adds.

What actually happened was that at about six a.m. she bounced out of bed, yelling, 'It's the holidays, it's the holidays, get out of bed, I've got it all planned Vinny!'.

I tried to roll over and ignore her but she was far too excited.

'Even the homework I have to do won't ruin things. I'll do it fast and have six whole weeks of watching daytime telly. We can rush around and tidy up just before Dad comes home for lunch to check on us.'

Right on cue Dad popped home, had lunch and sat and watched a bit of TV with us, then he went back to work. I had to remind her that we are supposed to do a little bit of study in the day; it isn't school homework, it's work Dad and Mum have set for us. She normally gets spellings to learn and I do some maths. Sofia rarely bothers to do it and they often forget to check the work anyway.

We sat and watched all the kids' programmes about making things – but hardly ever made anything as we never have any of the right stuff and we've certainly never found the sticky-back plastic shop either (which you need to make anything at all it seems). Though I did copy down a recipe or two, especially the cake ones.

Sofia is up early again and she's ready for a big adventure she says. She runs through to the living room to flick the TV on so she can check the weather.

She stomps back into the bedroom.

'The weatherman says it's going to be rubbish all week,' she grumps. 'I don't think we're going to get out to the park.' The thought makes me feel very grumpy too, even we can't watch that much TV.

'Those damn girls Abby and Pinkie are really lucky. They're on holiday in a hot country at Sarina's wedding for what, the entire holidays?' she quizzes me as I grab a bowl and pour in some Cornflakes.

'Yep, all of Sarina's family and all Abby's family too, the whole tribe are there all summer. I think about twenty-five of them are flying out. I hope the wedding is as good as Sasha's was.'

The furthest we're going this summer is Southend. We're going for the day and it's a really big treat and we do love it, but let's face it, Southend isn't exactly hot or exotic. But we're excited anyway. Mum always makes the best picnics and Dad always tries it on and says he would rather stay at home writing. A chance to get some peace, he says, but Mum won't have any of it. She makes him come and he always enjoys it in the end.

'Whoops, I forgot to fill in my diary. I'll have to squeeze in as much as possible today or I'll be for it!' She dashes off to find her crumpled diary.

I dump my breakfast bowl in the sink and turn on the computer. Talking about Sarina's wedding has made me think again about Abby's situation. I decide I need to know more about arranged marriages and the Internet seems a good place to start.

20

The days roll by faster than I want them to. We're fast running out of biscuits, and the house is a tip, Mum says. We do our best to have fun and not make a mess after she says this but hey, we're just kids after all.

The weatherman said the sun would begin to shine this week and it has. The days have become hot and lovely – thank goodness as I can't take much more of Sofia's whingeing. So we spend much more time outside, mostly at the park. I think I'm a bit too old for the swings but I like hanging out there and when no one is looking I have a swing.

Lots of kids from our school are there too but not Abby and her brothers and sister of course. I miss her a lot and wonder how she's getting on.

As though she's read my mind, Sofia calls out from the swing: 'Hey Vinny, won't it be great to show off our tans to Abby?'

'No, she wouldn't be impressed by that; anyway it will be much hotter where they are.'

We've not even been able to text as she wasn't allowed to take her phone with her. But I was hoping she'd have sent a postcard by now. It's driving me mad that we haven't heard from them. Every day Sofia races to the door when she hears the postman. I'm usually super patient but even I find an excuse to be at the door every morning hoping to find a postcard. I'm sure the girls will send us news soon, soon…

The weather stays good for another three weeks straight and

as long as we can go to the park and have some ice lolly money we are happy just to mooch around the park and meet Dad at home for lunch. We don't do anything special except when next-door-aunty treats us to a day trip to the zoo which is brilliant. I think we see every single animal in that zoo!

The holidays have passed by way too quickly, and six weeks have mysteriously melted away and we've less than a week to go. The weather changed this past week and we are back to spending our days indoors.

As we sit down to dinner Mum and Dad surprise us by announcing a trip to Southend tomorrow. It isn't much of a surprise, we knew we'd go sometime in the holidays but not when. We assumed it would be a weekend but they've decided to take the day off work.

'The weather's meant to be changing back to sunny, it will be twenty-three degrees tomorrow so we have to go to the beach and make the most of it.'

After dinner Mum packs an amazing picnic. It all smells so nice I want to eat it before we've even left home. She's made her speciality of part-boiled, part-fried aloo, potato, puri and chana (fried roti and chickpeas). She's also made some halwa and prepared a large tub of fruit salad with mangoes and strawberries.

'It's so not fair, I wish it was tomorrow already,' Sofia says, pouting.

'It's not long to wait and then beach, here we come!' Dad says, unexpectedly jolly for someone who normally wants to use the day to stay at home and write.

'Let's get up really, really early and go at five o'clock, Dad?' Sofia shouts, slinging her arms around Dad's neck and jumping on his lap.

'Maybe not that early,' Mum protests.

'Sounds like a fantastic idea,' Dad says winking at Mum and me. 'You'd better get off to bed Sofia, if it's such an early start you want.' And for once Sofia skips off to bed without any complaint.

By the time Sofia gets up, we're already sitting at the table eating breakfast.

'Hey, what happened to five a.m.? We've been waiting for you,' says Dad, tapping his watch with a smile on his face. Sofia squeals when she realises how late it is. It's then like a military operation, with Sofia in command of course, getting all our beach stuff packed before we can leave.

We catch the bus to Liverpool Street station. Sofia is on a complete high. We've barely pulled away from the platform when she asks, 'When will we be there?' I put my earphones in and do my best to ignore her.

Dad settles down to read last weekend's paper and Mum borrows the travel section off him. She also pulls out the comic section for Sofia who then begs me to read it to her.

'You're very capable of reading it yourself,' I say, turning up my music and going back to looking out the window, watching the skyline change from tall tower blocks to suburban semis.

At last we arrive and haul ourselves out of the carriage at Southend. We emerge from the station to glorious sunshine. Briefly, the day seems perfect until the moment is spoiled by Sofia dropping her rucksack on my feet.

'It's way too heavy. You hold it,' she demands.

'No way. Why did you bring so much stuff anyway, you little pest? What on earth have you got in there?' I snap.

'Now now, come on, this is a treat so let's not spoil it,' Mum says picking up Sofia's bag herself.

'Can we go straight to the funfair please?' Sofia asks, smiling up at Mum and Dad like some sort of cherub.

'But I want to go to the beach first,' I interrupt.

'I think we should go for a cup of tea,' sighs Mum, steering us all towards a café.

After tea and cakes Mum declares it is time for the beach. Southend beach is crowded, heaving with people making the most of the roasting hot day. Sofia holds on to Mum and Dad's hands as we slip down towards the beach. Once we find a good spot – well, one that Mum likes – we drop our bags and lay out our beach towels.

With the sunny blue sky above us, the sand under our feet and a gentle breeze coming off the sea, yes, all in all it is a perfect day.

Mum, Sofia and I lie lazily on our brightly coloured beach towels while Dad hunts down a deck chair to hire for the day. At one point Sofia changes into her swimming costume and runs straight into the sea, and then straight back out again screaming and making us all laugh.

'It's freezing!' she squeals, jumping onto my towel and spraying my book with sand.

'Get off, you're soaking me and getting sand all over my stuff.' Dad peers over his paper at us and smiles.

The best was yet to come of course and at the right hour – 12 noon to stop Sofia's complaining – we unpack and eat Mum's feast of a picnic. The afternoon is blissful. With full bellies we sunbath, build sandcastles – you're never too old, and they need me to dig the moat – and eat ice creams. As the sky begins to turn pink we start to pack away in the last of the warm sun.

'I can't get this sand out of my toes,' Sofia moans. 'It's everywhere.'

'What did you expect to find at the beach, Sofia?' I say sarcastically.

'You can have a shower when we get home,' Mum says, shaking the sand out of her bag.

But Sofia soon forgets about the sand when Dad points out that the funfair lights have been turned on and the music has started up.

'I think that's our cue for some fun, girls,' he declares.

We walk towards the rides and Mum puts our bags in a locker while Dad buys wristbands so we can go on the rides.

'I love the big wheel, let's go on that together,' Sofia shouts excitedly, dragging us over to stand under it. Moments later we're high above the fairground enjoying the sights below.

Next Dad points to the bumper cars.

'Who's going to be my partner,' he calls out, dashing ahead

of us.

'Me, me, me,' shouts Sofia, trailing behind him.

'It looks like it's you and me together then Mum,' I say. 'Let's go.'

The bumper cars are great fun. Sofia and I both drive. We laugh and scream as we crash into each other. Sofia and Dad end up in the tyre wall at one point, so of course I drive our car straight into them. We stumble off the cars with Mum saying she aches where she's been bumped and she'll never do it again. She says that every year.

A few rides later and it's time to go home.

'Please let's stay longer,' Sofia begs.

'No darling, it's already so late and we need to get the train home,' Dad says firmly.

'But it's not fair, I love it here, please let's stay longer.' Sofia is relentless sometimes.

'Come on, don't argue with your father. Let's get some hot donuts for the train,' Mum says taking Sofia's hand and leading her toward the warm sugary scent of the donut stand.

On the way home, I feel bone tired and am happy to lean back against Mum. There aren't many seats so we're sitting apart from Sofia and Dad. It's nice to be able to chat for once without Sofia interrupting.

I've had a lovely day and I suddenly feel guilty to realise I haven't thought of Abby all day. As soon as I do though, it recasts the shadow that has hung over me ever since that day in the park, a shadow which not even a sunny beach day can banish forever.

'Mum, do you think we will ever see Sarina or Abby again?'

'What do you mean, darling?' Mum asks drowsily.

'We've got used to having the girls around and I miss them, plus I'm worried about how it's going for Sarina. I keep asking Dad when they are coming back. But he says he doesn't know. He's usually the font of all knowledge.'

'Mmm, I don't know darling,' she murmurs.

'It's just I've been doing some internet research on arranged marriages and well, it seems that there is a big difference between an arranged marriage where the girl and boy get to decide which of the people put forward they will marry. Like Sasha did. What happened to Abby's sister, Anna, I'm pretty certain counts as a forced marriage and, well, it's not so unheard of is it? Girls go missing like this all the time, just like Tara Tally from my school. They just go on holiday and while they're away their parents force them to marry.' Mum opens her eyes now and I see that they're full of concern. 'And you know Anna never came back to England after her wedding and now I haven't heard from Abby at all. I thought she would have emailed, or at least written; it's been weeks since she left.'

'They may not have the internet in their village,' Mum says, stroking my hair. 'I can see you're still worried about her though. Let's you, Dad and I have a proper talk about this later after Sofia is in bed.'

The promised talk never happens: I fall asleep in the cab home from the station and go straight to bed.

21

The holidays have come to an end all too quickly and we're due back at school tomorrow. Still we've heard nothing from Abby and Pinkie.

I feel stupid that I don't even have an address so that I can write to them. All I remember is that they said they were staying at their dad's older brother's house in a small village.

I walk to school hoping to see Abby on the way, but I'm running late – Sofia dropped an entire box of cereal and of course I was the one to clean up – so I'm not too alarmed that I don't see her.

I slip into class just in time for registration for the new term. Our last year at this school and time for our final GCSEs before heading off to college. Miss Metcalf calls the register in much the same way she has with our form group since year seven. I look around the room and my heart sinks. All my worst fears have come true. Everyone is back and ready for their GCSE year; everyone except Abby Kambi. Somehow I get through the day but by the time I'm home I'm half mad with worry.

She still isn't in school by Friday of the first week back. This time, when Miss Metcalf reaches Abby's name during registration, she looks over at me.

'Vinny, you're a friend of Abby's, do you know why she isn't back at school as yet?'

'I know she went away at the start of the holidays, but I haven't heard from her since, Miss.' I answer, feeling guilty for some reason, perhaps because I haven't spoken up sooner.

'Miss, she was going abroad to a cousin's wedding,' Minnie

helpfully interrupts. Miss Metcalf nods sternly then dismisses the class.

I didn't tell any of the others of my fears so they really didn't know what was happening.

'Vinny, can I have a quick word before you go,' Miss Metcalf says as I push my chair in. The class shuffles out noisily leaving me behind staring awkwardly at the floor.

'Vinny, when was the last time you spoke to Abby?' Miss Metcalf looks serious.

'I saw her at the beginning of the summer holidays, Miss.'

'We've tried to contact her parents and we can't get hold of anyone.'

'Minnie's right, she went away for her cousin's wedding. She was meant to write to me but I haven't heard from her at all Miss, I promise…' Suddenly the strain of the weeks of worrying about Abby bubble to the surface and I begin to cry. 'I've been so worried about her and I just haven't known what to do. I told my parents and Dad has been trying to find out where they are – he even went to the restaurant where Abby's dad works and they said he wasn't back yet; they say he isn't due back for another week! But Miss, that's not all, before they left Abby's mum was really angry with her and let out that her father had a boy picked out for her as a husband. But Abby doesn't want to get married. She's too young. I'm worried Miss, what can we do?'

'Come on, dry your eyes, I'm sure Abby is perfectly alright,' Miss Metcalf reassures. 'I've a meeting with the Head to discuss this so in the meantime let's just assume all's well and her parents forgot to let the school know they'd be home later. Thank you Vinny, you can go now.'

'Should I go round to her flat after school, Miss? Just to be sure she's not home.' No matter what Miss Metcalf says, I feel I have to do something.

'No, that won't be necessary. Thank you though.'

As I rush out of the classroom I bump into Minnie who's been lurking by the door.

'Why did Miss want to see you?' Minnie demands.

'Nothing really, she just wanted to ask if I knew anything more about Abby.'

'Huh, well I'm Head Girl. She should have asked me.'

'Well I guess she asked me 'cos I'm her friend.'

'Where is she then?' Minnie retorts.

'Uh, I don't know, I haven't seen her all summer.'

'You're a really good friend then aren't you!' Minnie sneers before storming off. I feel my face redden with embarrassment. She's right, I haven't made enough of an effort to find out where Abby is.

As promised, during break Miss Metcalf went to speak to Lynne Andrews, the Head Teacher. With a feeling of foreboding she retold her conversation with Vinny.

'I think we may have a serious problem, Lynne,' Miss Metcalf said. 'Abby Kambi hasn't returned to school this term and none of her friends know why. The office has tried to contact her parents but there is no reply. I've been told she went abroad to a cousin's wedding at the start of the holidays. I even popped round to the Kambi's flat yesterday and made some discreet enquiries but nobody has seen them for weeks. Furthermore, I was alarmed to find out from Vinny that Abby's elder sister, Anna, was taken out of school when she was fifteen. I checked it out with her former school and the information is correct but they haven't been able to confirm what happened to her. Vinny says Abby told her she was tricked into getting married abroad. Abby is not allowed out after school and when her parents found out she was going to the science club they made her stop.

'I've spoken to some of her teachers and she's only been with us for one term but even in that time they have seen a change in her. She's always been very attentive but at the end of the term she became very withdrawn and she once hinted that her father actively discouraged her from doing homework. Lynne, I'm really concerned that Abby will not be coming back to school.'

Through all this Lynne was nodding with slowly dawning concern and taking notes. Then she looked up at Sue Metcalf.

'You're thinking of last term's INSET day, aren't you?'

'Yes, there was a speaker from Freedom Charity,' Sue answered. 'She said that schools can and should play a part in preventing forced marriage. That we should be aware and vigilant to the signs of forced marriage, and that the summer holidays are a common time when students are taken abroad and forced into a marriage.' Sue sighed. 'I don't know, Lynne, she may well just be absent without permission but it rings alarm bells for me.'

'I take it the office sent a letter home as well as calling?'

'They have, but there's still been no contact from the family. I've been re-reading the information Freedom highlighted as key warning signs.' Sue looked up from her bundle of notes with a worried frown. 'All of the facts relating to Abby Kambi are classic warning signs according to Freedom. What a shame I didn't get the chance to do a lesson on this with the children. I have it planned for this term.'

'Right, from the information Vinny's father provided, the family isn't due back until next week, so Abby's not missing as such yet. However, your gut instinct plus the evidence from Freedom is enough for me, I think we need to alert the authorities and set up a case conference.' Lynne picked up the phone. 'Let's cross our fingers that we're wrong and this is simply a matter of an extended holiday and not anything more serious.'

* * *

Minnie, Alex, Sheila and I are all sitting on the bench outside the snack bar.

'Miss Metcalf wants to know if anyone has seen Abby,' Minnie says.

'What's that all about?' Alex asks, not looking up from his iPhone.

'You're not supposed to be using that in school, Alex,' Minnie hisses.

'Whatever,' Alex shrugs.

'Well, we should go round to Abby's house tonight,' Minnie orders.

'I'll check her Facebook page,' Alex says, tapping away on his phone.

'She's not on Facebook, her life's not like everybody else's,' I remind him.

'Okay,' says Alex, 'let's do it the old-fashioned way then; go to her house.'

After school that day, I can't resist going to Abby's flat with Alex and Minnie even though I am pretty sure she isn't there and have been told by Miss Metcalf not to go there.

Alex peers through the letter box. 'All I can see is a mound of mail on the doormat, along with piles of leaflets and free newspapers.'

'It doesn't look like they've even come home from holiday yet then,' I say sadly. We walk slowly away from Abby's front door.

Opposite, one of Abby's neighbours peers through some shabby-looking net curtains. Minnie runs over to her door and knocks loudly. She's always so fearless, I think that's why she's my friend even though she can seem too forthright at times.

'Hello? Hello!' she shouts. Finally an elderly man answers.

Slightly embarrassed, Alex and I walk away, trying to disassociate ourselves from Minnie. She runs to catch us up.

'I asked the nosey neighbour but no one has seen anything of Abby and her family for two months now. He told me someone else came looking for Abby earlier in the week too,' Minnie adds, catching her breath.

'It doesn't look good,' I say quietly.

'What do you think has happened to her?' Alex asks, paying attention for once.

'They probably just decided to extend their summer holiday and forgot to get permission from the school,' Minnie suggests, but no one believes that explanation for a second.

'She'll be in big trouble with the teachers when she comes back,' Alex muses as the three of us drift towards the park. I don't feel like hanging out so I say my goodbyes and head home feeling like there's no hope at all.

22

I go home and immediately fire up the computer. I need to find out more about forced marriage and what to do if you suspect it has happened. I find one horror story after another.

The stories I read of girls that are forced into marriage are more horrific than I could imagine. There is one girl who was kidnapped and taken abroad, she was forced to marry some really old man. He beat her every day and eventually when she refused to do what he wanted, he threw her down a well and killed her.

Another case was where a girl's own dad killed her for dating a boy; he said she was too "Western".

There are so many examples and with each I feel more sick, my stomach turns over. I am shocked by how many examples there are.

By the time Dad comes home I'm in a real state.

'Oh darling, the last thing you should do when you're worried about something is to randomly surf the net. You can end up with inaccurate info and really get yourself worked up,' explains Dad. 'Look, I spoke to your head teacher today.' I glance up at Dad. 'Yes darling, I have been trying to make some enquiries and make sure the appropriate people are informed about Abby. Mrs Andrews suggested that if we do want to find out more ourselves we should look up the website of Freedom Charity. Maybe that's something you can do in the morning once you've calmed down a bit.'

I get up early Saturday morning to check out the charity website Mrs Andrews has suggested. Mum is up too, bustling around the kitchen making breakfast as I read up on what Freedom Charity does.

Sofia soon emerges from our room and immediately starts flicking through the TV channels. 'There's only news on. The news is boring. Every fifteen minutes they repeat what they just said. And, there's more violence on it than on WWF and you say I can't watch that,' she complains loudly.

Dad wanders into the room now, whistling while he towel dries his wet hair.

'What are you doing, darling?' he asks, peering over my shoulder. 'Ah yes, I had a good look at that last night.'

Sofia starts doing what she always does when there's nothing on TV, pounding Mum's scatter cushions, when suddenly she shrieks.

'Vinny, Vinny, quick your school's on TV,' she shouts.

By the time we dash to the living room, the news item is over and because Sofia was so busy shouting for us she's missed the story too.

'Drats! You missed it,' she sings, jumping up and down on the sofa.

'Are you sure it was my school,' I ask.

'Yes, do I look stupid, I know what your school looks like. Don't worry, it always repeats itself – that's why it's so boring,' she says, drawing out the word boring as she flops back onto the sofa.

We sit quizzing Sofia about what she can remember about the story. But Sofia's right, fifteen minutes later the news item repeats itself. Dad pulls Sofia closer to him on the sofa, probably to keep her quiet, but she looks chuffed with herself for noticing the news item in the first place. We listen as the reporter explains how police have just rescued a fifteen year-old-girl at an airport, moments before her parents were boarding a plane with her with the intention of forcing her into an overseas marriage. The cameras then switch to a shot outside my school and the reporter explains that they are still looking for another girl who has not been seen for several months. A photo of Tara Tally is shown.

'That's the girl from my class who disappeared, remember Mum, I told you, look they're showing old shots of when it happened and the police were in our school.'

'Was she kidnapped then?' Sofia asks, not really understanding what is going on.

'Sssh,' Dad urges her softly. He turns up the volume and we listen to the rest of the report.

'Tara Tally was taken out of school at the end of the 2009 winter term. The school initially assumed she was on holiday but she never returned and there was no explanation from her parents. At the time there were rumours that her uncle and father had kidnapped her and taken her abroad to be married against her will. The British High Commission have since discovered she was taken abroad to be forced into marriage and to add further mystery to the story, her parents have disappeared too. The police have detained two men for questioning in connection with the disappearances.' There's an accompanying shot of the reporter outside Tara's family house.

'So they didn't forget about her then,' I say quietly. 'The police kept on investigating.' I'm glad it wasn't ignored, that Tara wasn't forgotten. I just hope the same will happen for Abby, that someone will care, and care enough to do something. I squeeze Dad's hand. Now the reporter speaks directly to the camera.

'If you are worried you may be forced into marriage or you know of anyone who you think may be at risk of it, there is a way to get help. The details will appear on the screen now...' And while the reporter signs off, the website I've just been looking at appears on screen: 'www.freedomcharity.org.uk' I repeat out loud to everyone.

We sit there staring at the screen until the ads become too noisy and Mum switches it off.

I dash back over to the computer. 'Look Dad, there's even a checklist about forced marriage.' I run my finger down the list as I skim read it.

'Oh Dad, oh no, god no, all of these things on the checklist, it's all the stuff that's been happening to Abby lately.'

'Yes Vinny, I know.'

'Dad, you have to do something.'

'I've done all I can for now, Vinny. I've tried my best to get in touch with the Kambis and I've spoken with the local police, anonymously that is, to ask their advice in case what we fear is true.'

After dinner Sofia jumps up deciding to give us her own news report. 'The news at six,' she announces, and there we sit, a captive audience to her bulletin.

'The news at six, young girls are disappearing, bong. This is a report about the horrifying story of young girls disappearing and never being seen again. Bong, they are being taken abroad, and are forced to marry. Schools need to make an official report when young girls disappear from school, bong!' She looks very pleased with herself. Mum and Dad smile grimly, but I can't help myself.

'Sofia, this is real, it's not a joke you know and it looks like the same thing has happened to someone we know, don't you get it?' I rail at her. For once she looks ashamed.

'Sorry, I know I get carried away, I don't mean to,' she says quietly.

'Okay girls that's enough; it's been a fraught week,' Mum says. 'How about some hot chocolate and then it's bedtime for you, Sofia.'

We snuggle down on the sofa and sit in silence as we sip our drinks.

Come bedtime, Sofia makes the usual fuss but I feel so miserable I'm glad to go. As we lie in our beds Sofia says, 'Sorry, really Vinny, I didn't mean to upset you or seem like I don't care about girls who get kidnapped and stuff.'

I smile into the darkness. 'S'okay don't worry, Sofia, you're only ten, it's your job to be silly. Go to sleep now. Night.'

'Night Sis,' she says and very soon I can hear her soft snore. I face the wall and will myself to sleep.

23

Sunday morning is rainy and miserable outside, so with Mum and Dad's chores and Sofia and me having our first homework of the new school year, the plan is to stay indoors all day.

I finish my homework in double quick time. Sofia's playing in our room so I pick up the TV remote, planning to switch over to a repeat of Home and Away, when I hear Tara's name mentioned.

'Mum, Dad quick, they're talking about Tara again.' Mum and Dad hurry into the room and we all stare at the TV, hoping for good news.

'Tara's cousin and uncle have been arrested!' I say in astonishment, 'She'll be coming home.' But as the news story unfolds I realise she's still missing.

'I can't believe it, I thought they would find her...' My mind races back to the stories I'd read on the web and I look at Dad in desperation. 'Her uncle and cousin might have done something to her. What if they've hidden her or...or worse... Dad, what if they've killed her...'

Dad turns down the volume on the TV.

'I don't know,' Dad confesses, 'I wish I had some answers, but I just don't know my darling.' Even Dad looks beaten now.

'Why did she go abroad with them, why did Tara do that?' I question, already knowing the answer.

'Well, from what we've heard and seen on the news it seems she was kidnapped by her father and uncle. She may have just thought she was going on a family holiday. You've read the same as me online, it seems that usually the family don't tell the girl she is going to be married until the last minute, just before the actual wedding ceremony.' Dad replies.

'Yes, but her family are the one group of people Tara should be able to trust,' I wail. 'I wish I'd known her better; I could have helped her. Why couldn't her family just let Tara decide how she lived? And now Abby, I know her, I was her friend and I failed her too.' I begin to cry and Mum comes over to hug me.

'You've done everything you could,' she soothes, but nothing makes me feel better.

'But why didn't Tara tell any of us at school if she was worried? And Abby, why did she go abroad? She knew they were marrying off Sarina and they had a boy in mind for her. When you think about it, it was so obvious. She's not coming back, is she? Just like Tara, we won't ever see Abby again.'

'I don't know what to say, some families just get it terribly wrong, it can never be right for this horrendous crime against this girl, or anyone caught up in this.' Dad's helplessness is turning to anger now. 'Sometimes not even the parents of the girl involved can do anything to help. The family can be forcing them into it too. Often there are big things at stake such as money, citizenship and so-called "honour". Several months ago there was a case of a girl whose marriage was all planned. Her mum and dad saw how distressed their daughter was and changed their mind shortly before the wedding but were murdered when they went abroad to explain and to call off the wedding. The papers described it as a "dishonour crime", because these poor parents were murdered in cold blood, by the groom's family.'

I'm horrified. I can't remember the story, but then several months ago this whole issue was completely alien to me; it just wasn't part of my world. At that point, stories in the news were just that, stories that happened to other people in far off places. I take a deep breath, calming myself down.

'We have to do something, and soon,' I say. Dad rests his hand on my shoulder.

'You're becoming so grown-up, you're seeing the injustices

and terrible things that go on and realising that we have to stand up to it, say it's wrong and do all we can to stop it happening to anyone else. I am sorry about Tara. And I will do all I can to help girls like her, starting with Abby.'

24

Three weeks into the new school year and Abby still hasn't returned to school.

Mum, Dad, Sofia and I are all out for a walk. It's a sunny afternoon but there's the chill of autumn in the air. We're having fun dashing about bumping into each other as we try to catch the falling leaves when in the distance we see a familiar sight that brings us to a sudden halt.

It's Pinkie, her mum and Abe. Pinkie's mum is struggling to hold onto them both.

'Pinkie!' Sofia shouts at the top of her voice. Sofia and I run over. We're full of questions, but stand there dumbstruck. Eventually I ask where Abby is.

On hearing Abby's name, Pinkie's eyes noticeably fill with tears. She gulps hard and looks down. No one answers. Dad and Mum have caught us up and they greet Mrs Kambi and the children warmly but Dad doesn't hesitate to politely ask about Abby, saying how concerned everyone has been about them all. Mrs Kambi mumbles something and Dad shrugs at us. Mum nudges him to not give up.

'You must all come over to dinner on Saturday,' Dad says to Mrs Kambi. 'I'm curious to hear about your holiday.' Mrs Kambi looks very uncomfortable. Her eyes are red and the dark circles under her eyes look worse than ever. But Mum too insists they come over and with that we walk off in opposite directions.

Saturday night arrives and the Kambis don't appear. We pester Dad and Mum to ring them to find out where they are;

it's a good excuse to have a feast Sofia says but Dad knows my motives are different.

It's weeks before we see any of the Kambis again and when we do they turn up at our flat completely unexpectedly. People often just pop in and expect Mum to cook dinner at the drop of a hat but fortunately Dad and Mum don't seem to mind.

Sofia jumps up on the kitchen worktop to look out of the window as soon as the doorbell rings. It's always been her lookout point, so she can warn Dad and Mum who's at the door. She hisses to me that she can see Pinkie, her mum, her dad, the snotty baby Abe, and the horrid brother, Addi.

'Drats, why did he have to come?' she grumps. 'We're not letting that so-and-so play with us.' I ignore her and rush to open the door.

Dad is just behind me, enthusiastically welcoming back the whole family.

'It's so wonderful to see you,' he says as everyone is ushered into the living room and offered seats. 'How was Sarina's wedding? I hope the trip home was good and everyone was well?' He plays the innocent, but quickly moves on to ask, 'But where is Abby?' Mr and Mrs Kambi look nervously at each other.

'Oh she's in the village for a little while longer, some family matter to take care of,' Mr Kambi answers.

I'm holding my breath, hoping the adults don't realise we're still in the room, and stop talking about Abby. Sadly, Sofia blows it. Miffed that Pinkie – who's clinging to her mum – doesn't want to play, she starts to complain and nag. I can see Dad doesn't want to take the conversation any further with us there so he asks if Mum and I mind fetching some tea and cake.

Later, after Sofia and I have cleared up, Mum suggests us kids should all go play in our bedroom. No one moves.

'Go on; show them your new game,' she says more firmly. I'm desperate to stick around to hear what the Kambis have to say about Abby; Dad is sure to question them further, but Mum is staring at me furiously now and there is no getting around her.

So off we all reluctantly shuffle to our bedroom. Addi is nearly eight and quite a tall boy. He has hair so short he looks like he's been scalped. Pinkie still doesn't want to play and is unusually quiet. She is clearly unhappy about something and sticks to me like glue.

We play cards and I show them my magic tricks. But I think even Sofia notices the uncomfortable tension as she refuses to tie the baby Abe up in bandages as we had so much fun doing before.

'Tell me about what happened to Abby,' I eventually whisper to Pinkie.

She looks down again, fiddling with the playing card in her hand.

Sofia pokes Addi and with less patience asks, 'Where's your big sister?'

'It's none of your business,' Addi announces.

Sofia pokes her tongue out at Addi. He gets annoyed and goes back to the living room.

'So where's Abby?' I ask Pinkie more forcefully.

'She's not come back; she's been left out there,' Pinkie says, starting to sob. Sofia calmly puts an arm around Pinkie's shoulders, but I'm shaking with fear and rage.

'Why?' I ask, praying the answer isn't what I already know it will be.

'She's getting married,' explains Pinkie in a very quiet voice. 'It's all arranged. After Sarina got married they said it was Abby's turn. It was a waste of money her coming back on a separate trip to be married in a few months when she could just stay with Uncle Taj and be taught how to cook properly and learn the language too.' I stare at Pinkie in horror. Pinkie carries on but it is hard to understand her between all the sobbing. I catch the last thing she says though.

'She's marrying our cousin Ras.' She pulls a photograph of

Sarina's wedding out of her pocket.

We had momentarily forgotten about Sarina with all the worry about Abby. Sofia's eyes nearly pop out of her head.

'Who's that guy?' Sofia squeals as she points at the photo. Standing next to Sarina is this hunk of a guy; tall and very handsome.

'That's her husband, Jas' says Pinkie, whose tears are subsiding now.

'Wow! She landed a gorgeous guy, he's so fit.' Sofia fake swoons and laughs. But she soon realises she's the only one laughing. Pinkie frowns at her and points to Sarina in the photo.

'Stop it, she's not happy at all, it doesn't matter what he looks like, she just didn't want to get married yet,' Pinkie cries. 'She didn't have a choice because my dad's older brother decided it was the right thing to do.'

'Which one is the guy Abby's supposed to marry?' I ask.

'There,' Pinkie says, pointing out Abby's intended.

'What!' Sofia's jaw drops. Sofia and I are speechless, but for entirely different reasons. I am shocked that there is a real live man, not merely a boy, picked out for Abby to marry, while I can see Sofia is just thinking, 'hunk alert'. Ras is Sarina's husband's twin brother.

'So what does Abby say?' I ask, which sets Pinkie off crying again.

'She's dead scared,' she says between tears, 'and she begged Mum and Dad not to leave her. She promised to be good if they let her come home, but Dad's brother said no. She promised to do all the cooking and cleaning and she promised to look after all the kids, she promised and promised. But they wouldn't listen. She wants to come back to school, but Dad said no, that it's a waste of time. I don't understand though. Your dad always told us it wasn't a waste of time, that education is important but what use is that if our dad won't listen?'

Pinkie tells us the twins both work in their father's garment factory and are rich, but that they don't keep servants because the women in the family are there to slave for them day and night and now they have Sarina and soon will have Abby too. Apparently the brothers didn't want to get married either, they thought they could get Bollywood movie star girls to marry them, but they had to do what their dad ordered them to do. But they certainly didn't want Western girls full of ideas of freedom and choice. These young men have been spoiled, with all of the women of the family attending to their every need all through their lives and they have nothing in common with Sarina and Abby. Pinkie says they just bark orders at Sarina and Abby, expecting them to stay at home all day and certainly at night.

'Wives have no freedom at all. They can only do what their husbands tell them to.' Pinkie looks exhausted and beaten.

From what Pinkie has said I figure it isn't the brothers' fault really, it is just the way they've been brought up. Though admittedly they could have been kinder to Sarina and Abby. Sofia clearly hasn't grasped what's going on because she says, 'I don't get it, why are they so unhappy? These guys are really good-looking; they look like models.'

'Abby doesn't care how he looks, don't you get it, she's only fifteen, she wants to be at school and to have some freedom, she doesn't want to get married!' I turn to Pinkie, exasperated at Sofia. 'What do your parents say?'

'Mum keeps crying when she thinks I can't hear her. She doesn't say so, but I know she wants to bring Abby back home before she marries. She wasn't ready for this, but Dad says that if she comes home now she will shame the family.

'Dad's older brother, Uncle Taj, was like a father to him, so he says it would be wrong to go against him. Besides, they said Abby was already there now and it would be too expensive to fly her back and forth.

'They probably had it planned all along, they were never going to bring her back, and with the attention on Sarina, nobody thought to be concerned for Abby.' Pinkie says. I am really shocked how grown up she is, compared to Sofia.

'Abby said she would kill herself if they forced her to marry

Ras but Dad told her not to be so dramatic,' Pinkie says, crying really hard now. 'Oh Vinny, it was so awful. They didn't tell us they were leaving Abby there until the day we left. I had a plan, that we would hold onto each other so tight they couldn't separate us and Abby would have to come home with us. It was only on that morning that we even knew we were leaving because Mum started packing our stuff up, though she didn't pack it all as she left most of it for our cousins out there. Then at midday, the hottest part of the day, we heard a car pull up. It was Uncle Taj and we knew that the time had come. Abby and I went and hid in the garden, behind the mango tree.

'We could hear everyone calling for Abby, and I got really scared, especially when my dad shouted for me to come. But I held onto Abby, then I saw Addi looking down on us. Abby begged him not to tell the others that he had found us, but he just looked at us, smiled, then shouted at the top of his voice.

'Suddenly everyone was surrounding us and hands were pulling and slapping us. Mum was crying but she too was trying to pull us apart. Uncle Taj was getting angry as the car was waiting and Dad was shouting, but we held onto each other as tightly as we could. Abby begged Abbu to let her go home with us, then finally he said she couldn't come because he didn't even have a plane ticket for her, that she must stay and get married. Then, as everyone was shouting and screaming, Mum moved close to whisper in Abby's ear. I thought she was going to help her but she spoke quietly and calmly, and then...' Pinkie broke into sobs again. 'Then all of a sudden Abby let go, she just let go...'

I'm stunned and can't imagine what their mother could have said to have made Abby give up like that.

'Abbu just picked me up and dragged me into the car, hissing to me that I was bringing shame on him. But I never gave up. I was still screaming and trying to reach Abby. Vinny, that was the last I saw Abby and I don't think I will ever see her again in my whole life. Now I've lost two sisters.'

'We'll get her back,' I say, completely horrified but fighting back the tears and giving Pinkie a reassuring hug.

Sofia is silent but looks meaningfully at me and I know she's trying to show me that there'll be no more joking from her; she understands how bad this is.

'We don't want the adults to know we've been discussing this, we all need to pull ourselves together. Pinkie will be in trouble if her dad finds out she's told us,' I say sternly to Sofia. Then the horrible Addi marches in. I feel sick at the sight of him after learning of his betrayal.

'We're off now, so come on, get up,' he orders Pinkie. She glares at him but does what she's told.

'Hey Pinkie, we'll think of something, take care,' I say. 'See you soon.'

The moment the Kambis leave we run through to Dad and Mum and blurt out everything. The Kambis refused to tell them why Abby was staying out there for what they called 'a longer holiday' so they're keen to know what Pinkie said.

Mum has tears in her eyes by the time I finish and Dad is very quiet. Sofia settles herself on Mum's lap and Mum's knuckles turn white, she clasps her so hard. Dad turns to me and asks me to repeat Pinkie's story, so he can be sure of the facts. He tells me he can trust me to tell the truth and not exaggerate.

Mum and Dad say not much more about the matter and we go to bed that evening with little fuss or conversation. But neither of us can sleep and so instead we strain to hear the low tones of Dad and Mum talking, desperate to know what they're going to do about Abby.

'I will take this up again with Kambi. Abby is underage and they are forcing her to marry. It's illegal,' I hear Dad say.

I have to keep shushing Sofia. It was one question after the other: 'Would Dad mount a rescue mission? Would Abby be a slave?'

I lie in bed imagining what Dad could do and how horrible it all is for Pinkie too. Sofia rambles on, 'Dad always told us we should fight for what we believe in. I love fighting so that's good.

But how will fighting help Abby and Sarina? Maybe Dad could steal out in the middle of the night, get a helicopter to the girls' village, and fly them home?'

I'm tossing and turning, trying to block out her voice. Finally, I lose patience with her.

'Sofia, shut up and go to sleep!' I demand in a huffy voice.

'But do you think Dad will get a helicopter and go and do a midnight rescue to get Abby and Sarina back?' she asks hopefully. I sit up and turn on the bedside lamp so she can see how grumpy I am.

'No, of course not you idiot, not only can he not fly a helicopter but he can't just go out there, grab them and drag them back here.'

'Why, why, why?' she wails.

'Well, one, that would be kidnapping; two, how would he know where to go; three, how would he sneak the girls out without anyone seeing; and four, where would they hide when they got back? Oh, it's just hopeless,' I say, realising there's nothing Dad can really do, fantasy or otherwise. I fling myself back on my pillows.

'So what's going to happen to them then?' Sofia needs answers and I don't have them. I don't know and besides I still hope that none of this is really happening, maybe Sarina is okay and, after all, Abby isn't married yet, just living with her uncle's family. Maybe he will listen to her and let her come back.

Sofia will not shut up, she quizzes away until eventually Mum comes in. We don't have time to dive under the covers to escape a telling off. Normally we have a good five seconds notice; there is a loose floorboard that squeaks out a warning. But Mum surprises us. She has two glasses of warm milk on a tray and she's added two heaped spoons of drinking chocolate and topped it with marshmallows. Yum.

'Love you Mum,' we both say as we accept our drinks.

'Goodnight girls, love you too.'

We drink our sleeping tonic in silence and the chocolate does the trick helping us forget about everything for a while. Abby and

Sarina will be banished from our thoughts till the morning. Our dreams are all marshmallow coated as we sleep.

As we slept Mum and Dad talked well into the night. They were as shocked as Vinny had been. Mr Kambi had been very defensive and not at all keen to talk about Abby and then Mrs Kambi had seemed unwell and they went home. Dad did lots of research on what help was out there. He read the statistics on how many girls and boys had been rescued – for it happened to boys sometimes too – but not enough of these children ever came home.

Finally Dad shut down the computer, rubbing his tired eyes.

'It doesn't look good,' he said to Mum. 'The success rate of getting girls back once they've gone out of the country is quite low. The best hope, they say, is to alert the authorities before the girl is taken out of the country.

'The Foreign Office have to get involved otherwise and it's all very complicated, but not impossible. If there was just some way we could get her back into the country…what we need is a miracle.' Mum put her arms around Dad.

'I am going to have to speak to Kambi . It's going to be difficult, but if he doesn't bring Abby back, I will have to report him to the police, he simply must not be allowed to do this again.'

'I am sure he will see sense; let's keep on doing what we can. Don't give up hope. Let's go to bed and think about it again tomorrow.'

25

They say miracles come in all shapes and sizes and I'd add to that. Some miracles are mixed blessings and we are about to learn the truth of that.

The morning after the Kambis' visit, we sit eating our cereal in solemn silence. The phone rings and Mum answers before Sofia can reach it.

'Who is it, who is it?' Sofia demands. Mum mouths a shush. By the look on her face I can tell there's something wrong. All she says is, 'Oh no, I'm sorry, what can we do?' Then, 'Okay,' and she hangs up the phone.

'What?' Sofia asks, ignoring Mum's glare. 'What's happened?'

'It's bad news,' Mum says quietly and instead of telling us she walks past Sofia and me and goes to talk to Dad who's still in the living room. Sofia marches in after her, only stopping to pull me with her.

'It's not good,' we hear Mum say slowly.

'What's not good, Mum?' I ask.

'Wait in the kitchen girls, I need to talk to your father.' Why is she stringing this out? We give up and go back to our breakfast, but Sofia is muttering about it not being fair as usual.

Five minutes later Mum and Dad return to the kitchen. I know because Sofia is timing it.

'Five minutes is three thousand seconds, and that's ages to wait,' she whines.

'Shh, Mum and Dad will tell us now, Sofia.'

'Mrs Kambi is ill,' Mum says. 'Apparently she collapsed last night in front of the children, shortly after Mr Kambi had left for work. Pinkie had to run for her Dad as without Abby, they didn't know what else to do. He phoned for an ambulance and the poor woman was rushed to hospital while Mr Kambi was left with all the children crying and thinking that she was going to die. It must have been terrible for them all.'

'How bad is she?' I ask.

'They don't know yet, but Mr Kambi said they suspect it may be some form of cancer.'

Later in the day, Mum calls Mr Kambi back and offers to take some tea round for the children, but he says no thank you, Pinkie will handle things. I think how strange it must be in their house with both Abby and Mrs Kambi gone. Pinkie is far too young to be relied upon to care for everyone, but I know she'll try her best no matter how upset and scared she must be feeling.

* * *

In the Kambi household Pinkie stood in the middle of the kitchen surrounded by her failed attempts at making dinner for her family. Her father sighed at the sight and said they were having a takeaway. Pinkie, relieved that he hadn't lost his temper with her, even started to imagine a takeaway pizza with garlic bread. But no, they would call by the restaurant he worked at to get something from the kitchen.

The takeaway was oily and had too much chilli in but it was hot and filling and no one dared complain. The food seemed to calm and quieten the children but when they'd finished eating, the children were so tired they could no longer hold back their tears.

'Just get to bed, the lot of you and stop crying; your mother will be home soon,' their father yelled.

'I want Mum and Abby home,' Pinkie cried.

'Just get your brothers ready for bed and stop all this noise, you kids are sending me mad, you're too much trouble. Pinkie, I said get everyone ready for bed,' he barked, retreating to his bedroom and slamming the door shut.

'Shut up, shut up,' Pinkie pleaded, 'you kids are making Dad angry. Look I'm trying to help you.'

Addi started to cry again. 'I want Mum,' he wailed as Pinkie shoved him into the bedroom and flung his pyjamas at him.

'Get yourself ready, I have to look after baby Abe.'

Eventually they were all in bed, full of hot lamb curry and garlic naan but there was no mother there to remind them to brush their teeth or wash their faces. And although they stayed up late and got away with not having to do the usual boring bedtime routine , they were not happy. They were worried about their mum lying ill in the hospital ward.

The next day the Kambi children sat in a hospital corridor, waiting for news about their mother.

'It is no place for children,' the rather plump, old-fashioned ward sister had told their father, and so they couldn't see their mother and fidgeted miserably while they waited.

26

Lying in her hospital bed, Mrs Kambi wondered how the family were coping without her. She had just been told through a translator, that she'd been diagnosed with breast cancer. She feared the worst for herself and her family. How would they manage without her if she didn't recover?

Her usual routine at home was to get up a good hour and a half before everyone else and go to bed an hour later than everyone at night. Her day was filled with chores: washing, ironing, cleaning, organising the children and what they needed, making meals and packed lunches, tending to her husband's wants. Every day she would make a proper cooked breakfast of potato, roti, eggs and chai. And she never complained or moaned. She had known from a young age this was expected of her and had worked this hard since she was eight. Besides it had been easier while she'd had help from Abby. Her heart lurched as she thought of her. She wondered how Abby was coping in her new home.

Then Mrs Kambi realised that this stay in hospital was the most rest she could remember ever having had; she'd certainly never had a holiday.

With nothing to do but lie there with her thoughts and wanting to keep her mind off her illness, she started thinking back to when she was a small girl. She and her five sisters did all they could to help their mother with the household chores and even though they worked hard they always had fun too. The days were full of chores but in the evening their mother would give them handmade wooden knitting needles and they enjoyed long evenings of singing folk songs as they knitted.

'Ah,' she sighed at the memory, she missed her family but she wasn't a girl anymore and once she had married she didn't belong to them any longer and had to concentrate on her husband and rapidly expanding family.

The consultant had asked the translator to question her about her family medical history, the women's in particular. It was only then that it occurred to her that most of her female relatives had died young, including her mother and sister. Nobody had talked about it at the time, but on reflection perhaps they too had suffered from breast cancer. It would explain the silence around the illnesses and deaths. Mrs Kambi had been married very young. After her wedding day, she never saw her mother again as she had died within weeks of the ceremony, aged just thirty. One of her sisters had also died in her mid-twenties. As the translator ran through the consultant's questions and explained what would happen, Mr Kambi also stood there and she could see the fear on his face. But she couldn't know that he was also experiencing the dawning realisation of what had happened to her relatives and that he did love his wife and really it was only now he realised how much. What she did expect him to be worrying about were the practical matters to be faced. Mrs Kambi was to be in hospital for some time and they both knew he couldn't be expected to care for the children and house alone, even with Pinkie's vain efforts to help.

As Mrs Kambi feared, her organised home was complete bedlam in her absence. Monday morning had brought new problems.

'Come on, get ready for school. You do it every day; you must know what to do,' Mr Kambi yelled. 'You're all going to be late.'

'I can't find a clean shirt, and where are my trousers?' Addi screamed. 'Dad, Pinkie's not washed any of my clothes!'

'Shut up! Mum's only been in hospital two days, Addi!'

'Aah,' their father put his hands to his head. 'Just get dressed, now!' He'd never had to deal with such complaining and arguing before.

'We haven't got any milk, Dad, what shall we do for breakfast?' Pinkie asked. In all the pandemonium he had still not been food shopping. So there was no bread and no milk and no Mrs Kambi to make their usual cooked breakfast. He ordered Addi to go to the shop.

'Why me? Make Pinkie go,' Addi protested.

'Go,' his father yelled.

Half an hour later they sat around eating soggy cornflakes.

'Hey now, come on you will be late for school,' Mr Kambi bellowed. 'Pinkie, not you, you stay home today. Someone has to clear up this mess and look after Abe.'

As Addi scrambled from the table and followed his father out of the door, Pinkie was left literally holding the baby.

27

The day of Mrs Kambi's operation had arrived. They would be doing a complete mastectomy as the cancer was very advanced. She had phoned and begged to see the children before she was operated on; she really feared not living through the operation. Mr Kambi managed to organise this around his work shifts, but he dreaded bringing all the children with him on the bus to the hospital. They were just too much to control.

He dashed home from work to find Pinkie struggling to get the baby Abe ready. Pinkie herself wasn't ready and she cried quietly. She wanted her mum to do her plaits. Mr Kambi could only shout and plead with her and eventually they were at the school gates waiting with the rest of the children for the bus.

Their mother was pale and sleepy when they finally arrived at her bedside. The kids were silent; they'd never seen her in bed. She was always up before them and in bed after them. Pinkie looked at her mother looking so small and frail and couldn't help but cry again, which started them all off. Not one of them had a handkerchief to blow their noses on, except for Pinkie's dad, and he was the only one who didn't cry. Inside, though, his heart was breaking. His wife, his loyal wife, could be on the verge of leaving him. How would he cope? His mind was racing. The crying, wailing, sobbing and sniffing not only stirred up Pinkie's mum, but also the unwanted attention of the nursing staff. The staff nurse shooed the kids into the TV lounge and she gave them each a small chocolate, which they all at first refused, until Pinkie took charge and told the others they were allowed to have it.

The visit was cut short as it was time for their mother to go into surgery. She wouldn't be out for several hours, so Mr Kambi took his distraught family home. Even Addi appreciated the seriousness of their mother's condition now and in their small flat, his father laid out their prayer mats and they all bowed down to ask for their mum to be home safe and well.

The following day Mrs Kambi woke after her surgery feeling confused and alone. Her last thought before she went to sleep had been about her village and now she'd regained consciousness, memories flooded back of the young carefree girl she had once been. Thoughts she'd long tried to forget pushed forward and plagued her heart. She realised that like her mother and her grandmother she was married too young, always worked too hard and never had time to enjoy life and her family. She finally understood that she'd had her entire youth taken away from her.

As the morning went on Mrs Kambi became more and more distressed and lay there sobbing. The nurse couldn't understand anything Mrs Kambi was muttering and gave up trying. It was only when Dr Begum arrived that anyone was able to help and comfort her.

'Dear Mrs Kambi, please don't stress yourself so much, this is not going to help your condition.' But, inconsolable, she continued to cry trying to hide her face in her pillow.

Dr Begum sat on Mrs Kambi's bed, held her hand and patted it.

'Things will be okay, you just concentrate on keeping yourself calm.' Surprised at her affection and persistence, Mrs Kambi turned to Dr Begum. Mrs Kambi's eyes were red and swollen and looked up at the kind doctor's face with a helplessness Dr Begum often witnessed.

'What will I do, who will look after my children if I die? My husband… he cannot manage alone… My poor sister died so young and my Mumma, I lost her so early too, and now it's my turn to die. This cancer is going to kill me isn't it, the same way it killed them? And what is the point of such a short, hard life?' she asked.

Dr Begum was confused by the change in the conversation but she kept quiet and simply listened.

'I got married when I was too young, I had to work hard but my mother-in-law would still beat me because she said I worked too slow. But I'd grown up poor and had always done what I was told without question, without thinking there could be another way.

'Now I have done the same to my own daughters. I'll never see Anna again and I know she's beaten like I was. And Abby, poor Abby. She knew differently. She was happy and now we have left her behind in my village to marry. She has seen a different life to the one I knew, she has grown up here and so wants to be like her friends. I had hoped if we got her married young, she would resign herself to her fate but in my heart I know she won't give in.

'I made Abby work even harder in order to teach her, so she wouldn't be beaten like Anna and me, but all I've done is made her angrier, bolder and more determined. What have I done, forcing my poor daughters into this kind of life where they can never be happy and will die young? I want my girls home. But it's too late…it's all too late…' Mrs Kambi's sobs took over and she barely heard Dr Begum's reassurances.

'I'm sure something will be possible. As far as your health is concerned, we are treating the cancer aggressively and there is a good chance you will make a full recovery. Don't give up hope yet Mrs Kambi, please don't give up. I promise I'll do something.'

28

The phone rings and Sofia runs to answer it.

'Hello, thank you ever so for telephoning us, would you like to talk to me?' she enquires in her fake posh voice. There's a pause and then she says suddenly more seriously, 'Yes he is' and passes the phone to Dad who takes it into the other room so he can speak in private.

'It was Mr Kambi,' Sofia nods knowingly to me. At least for once she had the sense not to pester the caller with her usual silly questions.

Dad is on the phone for what seems like ages.

'Girls, Mum and I are off to the hospital. Next-door-aunty is coming over to sit with you Sofia. Vinny, would you mind coming too to watch over the Kambi children so their father can visit with us?' I nod and of course Sofia complains.

'It's not fair. I'm a great hospital visitor, I can go and talk to all the people who don't have visitors and…'

'Enough, Sofia,' Mum says, suddenly cross. 'I'm sorry, but it's not appropriate. Maybe next time.'

Mum put together some Indian food for Mrs Kambi guessing the hospital food might not be what she is used to: some kitcheree and yoghurt and a few sautéed jeera aloo (potatoes with little brown seeds that smell nice). Next-door-aunty comes over just before we leave and soon she and Sofia are playing cards; cheating at cards always cheers Sofia up.

We arrive at the hospital shortly after visiting hours have begun so it is crowded with concerned families and friends.

'Jaini?' Mum quietly asks Mrs Kambi as we approach the bed. Her face is turned to the window and as she moves to look at us we are shocked to see how ill she looks. She is thinner and paler and clearly terrified of what will happen if she doesn't get well soon.

'How are you?' Mum takes her hand.

'Ah, feeling a bit better, thank you,' she says, but there are tears in her eyes.

She is grateful for the home cooked food Mum has brought and the smell of it seems to lift her spirits a little. But it is brief as suddenly she breaks into tears. I look about awkwardly, not knowing whether I should continue to stand there, but Mum instantly sits down by the bedside and Dad looks about for some tissues. I just lean against the window sill and hope I'm not in the way.

'Oh Jasmine,' Mrs Kambi sobs, 'how is my poor husband going to manage? Pinkie's too small to do everything at home and I miss Abby terribly. How is my poor husband going to cope without me?' she cries covering her face with her hands. 'I don't understand what the nurses are saying to me and Abby is such a clever girl, she understands everything. Oh how could I have let her go? I love her so much but she'll never know that now.' Dad and Mum exchange surprised looks and I have to hold back from crying myself and begging Mrs Kambi to let Abby come home.

'She wanted to be a teacher you know but that will never happen. She'll just be a wife and mother like me and my mother before me. I've had lots of time lying here thinking about it all and I know that that way of life is... well, it isn't right for Abby.' She looks down at the tissue she now clutches in her hand.

'Maybe she will still find a way to be a teacher, if she could come home,' Dad quietly suggests. 'Positive thoughts are best, Mrs Kambi,' he adds with a soothing voice.

Then something I'm not expecting happens. Very quietly, Mrs Kambi says, 'Please ask my husband to bring Abby back. Please try, please. This could be my last request.' Dad's face doesn't flinch, he only says firmly but calmly, 'I will try my best, don't worry.' I look at Mum who is struggling to hide her relief – this could be the miracle we'd hoped for. Mum squeezes Mrs Kambi's hand harder.

'It'll be okay,' she reassures. 'You must just focus on getting better.' Mrs Kambi's eyes close and she seems to fall asleep. A doctor comes up at that moment and introduces herself as Dr Begum. Seeing Mrs Kambi asleep she's about to leave when Mum asks if they can speak to her about a private matter. They walk off to a separate room leaving me standing uncomfortably beside a sleeping Mrs Kambi, my mind racing with what she's just asked.

Later I learn that Dr Begum is not surprised by my parents' story about Abby.

She's heard similar stories of forced marriages and is already aware that Mrs Kambi is worried for her daughter's well-being. Dr Begum has already decided to report it to social services, telling my parents that it is her responsibility but she is relieved to hear our family is also trying to help. Before anything else happens and Dr Begum calls social services, Dad pleads for some time with Mr Kambi, he's certain he can get him to change his mind about Abby. Dad comes back to the ward and takes me to the TV room where the Kambi kids are sitting with their father.

'Vinny, will you watch the kids for half an hour please, I need to speak with Mr Kambi.'

* * *

Outside, on a damp bench, Nasir Kambi and Shekhar sat holding flimsy plastic cups of tea.

'The doctors seem pretty confident she'll recover,' Shekhar said. 'But how are you coping?'

'I just can't manage without her,' Mr Kambi confessed and for the first time since he was a young boy he broke down and cried. Shekhar waited and said nothing, respecting Mr Kambi's pride. Then he listened as the man offloaded all that he had been thinking and worrying about the past days. Finally he spoke.

'Listen, you need help. We will do all we can of course, but your wife will need a lot of care when she comes home from hospital, who will do that? You have to work and you have the children to support.' Dad took a deep breath. 'Why not bring Abby home? Everyone will understand. I can arrange a ticket for her if you wish, so long as you allow her to come home immediately.'

'It's not that easy Shekhar, what will people say?' Nasir said almost shaking.

'Look, I'll be honest with you, it's not just the care of your wife I'm concerned about. I'm concerned about Abby's welfare and there is another complication: the hospital. I'm afraid that your wife was so upset and confused following the operation that she told them what was worrying her and now they will have to report matters to the authorities. They'll contact social services.'

'But I've tried, it's not that easy...' Nasir started to interrupt.

'I don't think you fully understand what you've done, Nasir,' Shekhar continued forcefully. 'In this country what you've done is regarded as kidnapping. My dear Nasir,' Dad looked straight into Mr Kambi's eyes. 'Forcing your daughter into a marriage is a crime. If you insist on going ahead with this, you and your wife could go to prison for a long time. Up to seven years. Then who would look after your children?' Dad was firm and strong. Mr Kambi wiped his tears on his sleeve.

'The school has already reported Abby's disappearance. And if you don't bring her back, you will leave me no option, I will have to go to the police and tell them Abby is being kept out there against her will. I will tell them everything I know and so will the staff here.' Shekhar didn't mean to sound threatening, he was merely stating the facts. 'My friend, your problems will keep on growing and multiplying until they overwhelm you. Take action now; do the right thing.'

But earlier that day Nasir Kambi had tried to take action. He had already had several calls and visits from the school authorities and did not want the police involved. He wanted his brother Taj's advice and guidance.

Taj was angry when he answered the phone. He was at his wits end, he had no idea how to handle Abby; beating her, shouting at her, and still she was defiant, refusing to eat.

'Brother, talk some sense into your daughter,' he barked throwing the phone to Abby.

'Let me come home, Abbu,' she screamed.

'You bring shame on all of us, you stupid girl,' Nasir scolded her. 'You listen to your uncle and do exactly what he tells you. What is wrong with you? Are you ill, why are you refusing to eat? All this crying is no good, your uncle is a very generous man, don't upset everyone like this.'

'Please Abbu, let me come home,' Abby sobbed. 'How could you just leave me here? I will never do what they say, never. I am going to starve myself to death, and it will all be your fault.' Abby pleaded and begged until eventually Nasir demanded she put his brother back on the phone. He suggested maybe Abby should return to England, just until the wedding so she could help with her mother. But Taj was worried how it would look for her to return to England. And when Nasir mentioned the school authorities and his concerns that they would contact the police, Taj scoffed at him and said he did not believe the police would be interested in Abby.

In the end Taj's arguments won. Abby had not adjusted to life there and for her to return to England now would make it even worse come the wedding. Even Nasir agreed with that. He asked to speak to Abby one last time.

'I can't stay out here, please, just let me come home, please, Abbu,' Abby begged again.

'Abby, you have to listen to your uncle he knows best. I have enough to cope with here with your mother in hospital…'

'What! Why do you mention this last of all, why didn't you say immediately? What's wrong with her?' Abby demanded.

'She's ill, pretty bad…' Nasir started to explain, but before he could finish Abby heard the dialling tone. The line was bad again and the connection was lost.

'I have to call him back,' Abby said in desperation. 'What's wrong with my mother?' Taj just stared at her as if she were a nuisance fly he was considering swotting. Her pleas were pointless, Taj simply unplugged the phone and left the room with it clutched in his hand.

29

Abby kept a diary of every horrid thing that was happening to her; how she felt, how she was desperate to be home with her mum and her brothers and sister and how dearly she loved them. She kept the diary with her always and as she wore a burkha whenever she was outside, she could easily keep it concealed.

She had recently been to visit Sarina who was living in Uncle Richi's house with her new husband, Jas. Sarina was no longer bubbly and wearing her bright red nail varnish. She was silent, worryingly silent. Her bright smiling eyes were hollow and rimmed with a dull red. School now seemed so much more appealing than life here. Locked in, ordered to cook, clean and keep house. And all this in an atmosphere of fear. Her mother-in-law had quickly proven herself to be unkind and unrelenting.

'Are you okay, how are you doing?' Abby asked as they hugged.

'How do you think I'm doing? I hate it here and I hate them. Why are they doing this to me?' Although Sarina was whispering there was rage in her voice.

'I know, I hate it too, but Sarina, you agreed to get married, you knew this was going to happen to you.' Abby was confused and angry.

'I didn't agree, I just went along with it, I didn't think it was real, I just blanked it all out of my mind, hoping it would go away. And even if I had agreed, it's not like I knew what I'd be agreeing to. This is a living nightmare. No one will listen to me; no one will help me. I've even tried running away but I keep getting caught.' Sarina showed Abby her arms and back that were covered in bruises.

'My aunty beats me too, but I don't care. I will get out of here one day and when I do, I'm taking you with me,' Abby promises Sarina. 'There are organisations that can help. They have lawyers and stuff, I've seen them on TV. Vinny, she's my best hope, I know she will help us. She's intelligent and her parents understand, surely they'll alert them at my school and tell them about you too?'

When she was with Sarina, Abby's voice was fired-up and confident, but once back at Ras's home, she felt defeated again. She didn't really think she would ever be allowed back to England. She'd overheard Uncle Taj say to her dad that to let her return now would mean all this upset over again when she returned to be married. Plus he'd been concerned with the expense and what people would think. She knew that nothing could change Taj's mind. He was head of the family and unlike her father, whom he saw as being too soft on his wife and daughters, Taj was someone the whole family obeyed in fear. Abby knew her father had always been torn between the two cultures their family bridged. Nasir wanted his family to enjoy the riches of the West but to keep the moral standards he and his family before him had kept, and there was a high price to pay for this. His best friend, Khan, had left his country for England when he was just twelve. From that day on, Nasir dreamed of going to England too. Khan used to return to the village with suitcases piled high with gifts for everyone. Khan said he would one day open his own restaurant like his uncle had and Nasir could work with him. They would have the best of times.

Before he came to England, Nasir had worked with his brothers on their family's land. They worked from morning until night and they only ever had just enough to eat; no luxuries, just rice and fish. He worked with his brother Taj and when their father passed away Taj became head of the family. One brother, Richi, had the good fortune to marry a woman who inherited a garment factory so was quite well off. But Taj worked hardest of all and it was he who raised the money for his brother to go to England. He sold a small piece of their land to fund Nasir's new life in London where,

in Nasir's mind, the streets were paved with gold. Taj longed to live in England too, but he knew he could never leave his village, he was too old and too set in his ways. So Nasir was sent with Taj's blessing and he was to work hard and send money back home to support the rest of the family. For this, Nasir was forever indebted to his brother.

30

Nasir Kambi had visited the hospital every day since his wife had been admitted. This meant he'd missed three lunchtime shifts at the restaurant where he worked as a porter. He'd always hoped he would get promoted to a waiter's job or even shift manager, but his English wasn't good enough so he had to work back of house; washing, peeling and doing all the mundane kitchen stuff. But with Pinkie's help, he'd still been able to just make the late shift from seven in the evening until one in the morning. Nasir was particularly impressed by Dr Begum who seemed to take special care of his wife and it helped enormously she spoke their language. He was also impressed by her manner and how modestly she dressed, despite her Western education and profession. He listened to her and took note when she stressed to him how important it was that his wife had home support once she left the hospital.

But Nasir did not know that it was Dr Begum whom his wife had confided in about Abby. Dr Naz Begum had been patient with Nasir, resisting calling social services when she realised that she had a chance of talking him round. But it was hard to know what was best, She'd heard awful stories of children forced into overseas marriages through a barrister friend of hers. She knew the situation could end badly. She wanted Abby back too even though she'd never met her. It was over fourteen years since she'd been Abby's age, but she remembered only too well what it was like to be young and hopeful. Dr Begum was lucky. Her parents were reasonably wealthy and educated so they'd always had more options in life and they'd wanted the best for her too.

But she understood that many forced marriages were about favours, promises and money, so she wasn't quick to judge Mr Kambi. She was gaining his trust and respect and she hoped it would pay off soon because she'd sworn to his wife that she'd do something and she couldn't put it off much longer.

When Nasir returned to the ward following his chat with Shekhar, Dr Begum was waiting to speak with him. She took him to one side and politely informed him that social services and the school had concerns over the children, that they thought he might need some help. She was baiting him, leading him down a path. She didn't need to mention Abby, because within minutes he was wondering out loud about bringing his daughter home to help so that he didn't have to keep taking time off work.

'Yes, yes, you could bring her back,' she calmly suggested, as if the thought had never occurred to her. 'I think that would be a sensible solution.'

Nasir felt so much better. Of course he should bring Abby back, just until his wife was better. But then he thought of his brother. Surely Taj would understand. He would make him understand. For once he had to put his own wife and children first.

The following morning Nasir woke early to make the call to his brother Taj without the children interrupting. He had spent the night agonising about the best way to put the news to his brother. His tongue was all tied up; his stomach in knots; his heart in his mouth. He owed so much to his brother, he hated the idea of going against his wishes. As he picked up the phone his palms felt hot and sweaty. He dialled the number. His mouth was so dry he almost wished he wouldn't be able to get through to Taj, but after the long beeps the line was connected and he heard his brother's voice.

'I'm worried about my wife. I can't keep working while she is sick. I need Abby back home,' he blurted out.

'She is home, this is her home now,' Taj insisted.

'I can't manage without her, Taj. I can't go to work because I have to look after the kids. If I leave them on their own...well, my brother, it's not like the village, there's no one to look out for them, you just can't do that here. I've no choice and if our prayers are answered it'll be just until my wife is better.

'Before you say no again, understand this, Taj, people here will call the police if Abby doesn't return. I know that for certain. We will find a way to send her back soon without any of these problems. For now, brother, I am scared.' Nasir found himself holding back the tears.

Taj knew his brother couldn't cope, not with the worry of the police and Nasir needed to work to pay the bills, but he thought to himself that if Pinkie had been brought up correctly she should be able to look after the children. What with Abby crying and refusing to eat and Pinkie not even able to look after the family, all of this proved his brother was not strict enough. He had spoilt them.

'The airline ticket is going to be expensive, a complete waste of money,' Taj argued. But Nasir stayed silent, he wouldn't give way this time. Preparations needed to be made and soon.

Nasir borrowed the money for the plane ticket from Shekhar, who was happy to help, relieved and grateful that Nasir had finally seen sense. A flight was booked for the following Saturday afternoon.

When she heard the news, Abby's mum immediately showed signs of recovery. She sat up, looked brighter and even managed to eat a little solid food. Dr Begum could see a notable difference in her patient.

The children were not told what was going on during this whole time. They had been ignored throughout and of course thought the worst, that their mother was dying so they were doubly relieved to hear the news that their sister would soon be returning to her real home.

31

Abby was told she was going home just three days before her flight.

'You are only going back for a few weeks to take care of your mother and then you will return to get married,' insisted Uncle Taj. 'And you'd better be well behaved this time. None of this fuss or the shame it causes, Abby, just obedience,' barked her uncle. Abby nodded like a robot, but was fuming inside.

Abby managed to see Sarina before she left. Sarina was frantic, desperate to return with Abby, pleading, begging Abby to help her. Abby could only promise to do what she could.

The remaining days in the village felt longer than a lifetime. Abby continued to write in her diary, to keep her going.

I have to hold on. Uncle Taj hates me, I'm sure. He says I have brought shame on him because I have to return to the U.K. He says I am 'a wicked, useless girl who has cursed his family.' That I am spoilt and bad. His harsh words cut deep into me, but I don't bleed. Not now, knowing I am going to be free, going to see Mum, my poor Mum. Oh please Mum, please be okay.

Abby's prayers became more frantic, more fervently bargaining with her God, striking deals for her mum to be well and for herself and Sarina to be free.

But every minute of the nine hour flight home was a joy. Abby kicked off her shoes and swung her legs on to the spare seat next to her. She was in the seat next to the window, so Abby lay back in her seat, her head in the clouds. She ate every single thing that was offered to her and drank can after can of fizzy drink. She felt sick, but it was a good feeling. Every second that passed brought her closer to freedom.

Her father met her at the airport. She rushed to him but he brushed her aside. Despite allowing her home he was unhappy that he had been put in this situation, that she had brought him so much shame. Her return brought mixed emotions and though he desperately needed her help, he knew he had crossed his brother and would owe him even more.

Abby felt hurt but hid her feelings and insisted on going straight to the hospital. Nasir rushed back to work.

Mother and daughter clung to each other, scared to let go. They cried at being back together again and Mrs Kambi looked into Abby's eyes and said that no one could separate them now, that she would help Abby to achieve her dream of being a teacher.

The memories of Uncle Taj and his hot, claustrophobic house faded and died at those words. All that mattered now was that she was back where she belonged and she was never going back there. That she promised herself and now her mum was supporting her she knew it would be fine.

'Abby, I am so sorry, I was wrong, Abbu was wrong, we shouldn't have left you there. You were raised here, you couldn't handle a life so far away. And it doesn't make sense to send you to a place that we worked so hard to leave ourselves. I have had my life now and I want more for you than just cooking cleaning and rearing children. I know you are a clever girl and you want so much. I am sorry I scolded you so much. I love you. I wish I could bring Anna back home, but it's too late for her...' Mrs Kambi forced back the tears, she'd spent too long crying the past week and only wanted to look forward now, to a happier future. 'I hope Anna will settle and accept the life that we decided for her. I will always regret letting her go though. My life has been difficult but I am happy to have had you children, you are my life, my breath, now you are back with me, I will get better, I will protect you. I don't know how but I will stop Abbu sending you back, I promise you that much my dear.'

Abby stayed by her mother's bedside until it was dark and the nurses asked her to leave. She made her way back to the flat, happy to be back in the UK and to be able to walk down the road without men staring.

Abby was greeted with a whoop of delight from her siblings. They threw their arms around her. Pinkie was the most pleased because she too was being rescued; not from a loveless marriage but from the kitchen sink, from the cooking and the endless cleaning. The flat was littered with dirty socks and pants and heaps of washing. The children were hungry but Abby quickly prepared a dish of fish curry and rice. The one good thing about the ten weeks away was that her cooking skills had improved by leaps and bounds. After she finished clearing away the dishes, she settled down on the sofa and called Vinny.

32

'Hello, London calling,' Sofia says cheerfully, having grabbed the phone before me as always. I hover next to her.

'Hi, is Vinny there?' I hear a voice I thought I might never hear again. I snatch the phone from Sofia ignoring her protests.

'Abby, I don't believe it, you're back, oh my God, you're back!' I choke back tears of relief and happiness.

'Yes Vinny, it's really me. I've missed you so much...' Abby says there's too much to tell over the phone but that she'll come over tomorrow after she's visited her mum at the hospital. Abby's dad has arranged to do extra shifts at the restaurant, to make up for all the time he had to take off, so for once she's free to do as she likes – as long as she can bring the kids with her.

The next afternoon I rush to the door before I even hear the bell ring. I just sense that Abby has arrived. I throw open the door but am shocked by her appearance. She's so thin and her face is sallow and drawn. She just looks so tired, but her smile breaks my alarm and I see the familiar twinkle in her eye.

'I look rubbish, don't I?' she laughs. 'It's been like, the worst kind of nightmare but I'm back, I'm really back.' She bustles in with her brothers and sister in tow, Pinkie looking her happy self again. Abby barely breaks to take a breath as she continues chatting all the way through to the living room. 'And the best thing is, Mum supports me now, she doesn't want me to go away again. She wants me to go to college to train to be a teacher and everything.'

'That's amazing, Abby. Come on, let's go to my room,' I suggest. I go to close our bedroom door but Sofia slips in behind us. Thankfully, before I have time to argue with her, Mum marches in and pulls her out of the room, stopping first to give Abby a massive hug.

'We're so pleased to have you back,' she says. 'I'll bring back some fish and chips for a meal later. Sofia, I need you and Pinkie to come down to the shops with me now, your father's going to look after the little ones.'

'It's not fair,' she protests. But she knows it's no good. Mum has made up her mind, and anyway, her offer of chip shop chips is too much for Sofia to resist.

'Abby, don't worry; I won't be long and don't start gossiping until I get back,' Sofia yells as Mum slams the front door behind them.

'I'm sorry about her,' I apologise to Abby. 'Let's get a drink.' We go through to the kitchen. Abby sits down while I make us two milky coffees and dig out a packet of chocolate biscuits. We lean forward in our chairs, sipping our drinks, not really sure where to start, so much has happened.

'So how are you really?' I finally venture. 'It must have been terrifying.'

Abby is silent for a moment, then her eyes well up and as the tears trickle down her face she starts to talk.

'It's been awful, Vinny, worse than I would ever have imagined. And then when I found out that Mum was so ill, I had no one to talk to. Their lives are so hard out there that they're all so matter of fact about things; you just get on with life whatever it throws at you. So nobody cared that I was sad, lonely and scared about the prospect of getting married, and then really upset about Mum too.'

'When did you first realise you weren't coming back?' I knew a lot from what Pinkie had said but I needed to understand the full story.

'I thought I was coming back home right up until the last day. I'm so stupid to have trusted them. Dad and Uncle Taj had planned everything from the start. He tricked me into going over there because he knew I wouldn't have got on the plane if I'd known. Once Sarina's wedding was over, I heard him talking to

Uncle Taj about leaving me there because it was cheaper than taking me home and sending me back in a few months when I turned sixteen. In two months' time, Vinny, I would have been getting married if I was still there.' Abby shakes her head, still disbelieving how close she came.

'I know,' I say gently, 'none of us could believe your parents would do that to you. We had no idea either.'

'Sarina, Anna and I were just pawns for our fathers and their brothers. They truly believe they have the right to control our lives, they think they know what's best, but it's all about paying off old debts and gaining the most advantage in the family. The decisions they make over our lives are just imprisoning us and it's a cycle that must be stopped.' Abby takes a biscuit and seems to savour it more than normal.

'If Mum hadn't got ill Dad wouldn't have let me come back at all. I'm only here because he needs me to look after the kids and the flat. Women's work the men say! You know, I saw my sister at Sarina's wedding and she'd changed so much. She used to be such fun, she used to have so much life in her, but now she's scared of her own shadow. I didn't get to talk to her much, but she told me that I had to get away, to not let them send me back. Life is very hard for her and she hates Dad for forcing her to stay out there but now she's pregnant. She found out just before the wedding and she said it's changed everything for her. She said she wouldn't leave now even if she could because a baby changes everything and it's no longer all about her.' Abby holds her face in her hands and I watch her shoulders heave. 'Vinny, what could I have done to help her in time? I was only thirteen; I didn't have a clue what was going on and Mum never told us anything.' Abby is crying so hard it is difficult to understand everything she is saying. I try to comfort her but my words feel empty.

'She knows there's nothing you could have done. She doesn't blame you and she'll be pleased you've escaped the same fate. It's okay Abby, it's okay to be upset, you're safe now.'

'But Sarina is still stuck out there and I promised I wouldn't leave without her.' Abby looks up, red-eyed and desperate. 'It's not too late for her to come back, she's so scared, Vinny, she's terrified, she can't take much more. Vinny, we've got to do something.'

'We won't give up on either of them. None of it's your fault, none of it is, and you can do more for them now you're back here. We won't just leave them there though.'

'What can we do?' Abby stops crying and a fierceness comes into her expression. 'We must make a plan. Your dad will help won't he? Can we trust him not to tell my dad though?' Abby is scared that Sarina and Anna could get into worse trouble if we aren't careful.

'I know we can trust him and he'll think of something to help us,' I say comfortingly, hoping I can make my words come true.

We fall silent for a moment, finishing our coffees, then Abby suddenly says, 'They kept Sarina locked-up in her husband's house. She'd already tried to run away several times. She never got very far though and when they caught her they beat her black and blue.'

'Oh,' I gasp, 'Poor Sarina. Where would she have run to?' .

'That's the problem; she had nowhere to escape to. She asked the other women in the village to help her, but they just laughed and scolded her saying she'd get used to it, every woman did. But Sarina will never get used to it, I know I would never have got used to it either. Don't forget that her horrid mother-in-law would have been my mother-in-law too.' I shudder at the thought and wonder if Abby was beaten too. I don't ask; she'll tell me in her own time.

'Come on, eat up, you've become too thin, Abby,' I say passing her the biscuits. 'Did they not even feed you?'

'I refused to eat while I was out there. They couldn't force me to do that,' Abby says.

'You would have starved yourself, Abby?' I am shocked.

'You've got to remember they took everything away from me, Vinny, it was the only control I had left and…and…and possibly my only escape,' she stammers quietly. I can't bear to look in her eyes, they're so anguished, but she seems to want to talk about everything. Stories keep tumbling out of her experiences there and eventually we get onto the moment Addi betrayed her.

'Pinkie and I were crouching behind a tree, stupid place to hide really, and then Addi shouted out that he'd found us. To him it was like we were just playing hide and seek. He can be annoying but he doesn't understand, he just wants to please and be like Abbu.

'The next thing I knew everyone was shouting and we were screaming and I could feel hands hitting and pulling at me, then – it's like a bad dream now – Mum came over. It was as if time stood still and it was just me and Mum, she held my chin up to look directly into my eyes and she said,' Abby paused again, the horror of recalling the moment seemed to be too much for her. I held her hand and she carried on.

'I'll never forget a word of it. She said, "You know you have to stay, you have to do this for me, for your love of me." I nodded, of course I loved her. "You know our 'izzit', our honour is all we have and if I don't have that I have nothing, I won't be able to bear the shame. I will kill myself Abby, I will hang myself right here on this mango tree if you don't agree to do this. Think of your brothers and sister, you don't want to leave them without a mother. Stay quiet and be strong and do as we ask you."

'I couldn't speak, Vinny. I looked at her in disbelief. The family honour was that important to her. She had betrayed me too. I didn't care anymore, I just let go of Pinkie and sank to the floor. It's a blur after that. I remember Pinkie calling to me and then the sounds of the car pulling away and then silence. I stayed in the garden. It was dark but still I lay there and no one came. I couldn't move, I didn't cry, I felt dead inside.

'I know my Mum well enough to have known she wasn't just making idle threats. I couldn't do that to the little ones, what would happen to them? I was trapped. It was my happiness or theirs.'

'Your Mum was blackmailing you, Abby, you know that, don't you? How could she do that to her own daughter?' I say in horror.

'She wasn't blackmailing me really, she was just telling me the truth, Vinny, her truth, life as she knows it,' Abby says and I can't believe she's defending her.

'You don't hate her?' I ask wide-eyed.

'No, I don't hate her. In a strange way I understand why she did what she did, it's hard to explain how families like ours work, it goes very deep. And of course now I know that when she was lying in hospital, faced with the thought of death and of leaving her children behind, something happened inside her. She's changing Vinny, I don't expect her to suddenly be all modern but she knows how she feels about us girls now and she will help us I'm sure. I'm still getting used to the change. I'll tell you one thing, my life will not go the way they had planned, I will not marry until I choose to,' Abby finishes with conviction and I believe every word.

33

Jasmine dragged Sofia down the High Street stopping at every shop window, drawing the shopping trip out as much she could. They were gone for over an hour and a half. 'That's five thousand four hundred seconds' Sofia whinged.

When they returned, Abby had just left or Sofia would have bombarded her with questions. Vinny made Abby's excuses for not sticking around for the chips and Jasmine understood. Vinny curled up on the sofa with her bowl of chips to watch TV. She wasn't willing to tell Sofia any of Abby's news, so Sofia finished her chips and went to bed early in a huff.

As she threw herself onto the bed in frustration she landed on a little purple notebook that had slipped between the covers. Sofia quietly crept to the door, shut it, then turned on the bedside lamp and opened the book. It was filled with pages and pages of tiny neat handwriting.

Glancing briefly first at the closed door, Sofia began to read. It was Abby's diary. Sofia had never been a keen reader, but this was different. It was secret and it was something she knew she was not allowed to read. She couldn't put it down, even if someone came in now she knew she wouldn't be able to stop. She couldn't breathe. She was turning each page trying to read as fast as she could. Her heart was in her mouth as she read for over an hour.

She was so engrossed she didn't hear the floorboard squeak outside their bedroom. The door swung open, scaring Sofia half to death. Vinny saw her guilty expression and recognised the diary immediately as it was her gift to Abby before the summer holidays.

'That's Abby's,' she said accusingly. 'What are you doing with it?' Vinny snatched it out of Sofia's hand and charged out the room with it.

'This is private Sofia, don't ever look at what's not yours again!' she snapped over her shoulder. Sofia didn't even object, she knew she was in the wrong and unusually she was more concerned for Abby than herself.

Vinny had told Mum about the diary. As Mum walked into the bedroom she saw that Sofia was sad and subdued. She stroked her hair and kissed her goodnight. Before the door closed, Sofia let out a sob.

'But Mum, how can I, the diary, I can't believe it... Poor Abby. It's not fair! Real-life not fair...' For the first time in her life Sofia had a genuine sense of what wasn't fair and it wasn't about anything trivial.

Mum soothed her softly until Vinny came to bed.

Sofia sat up, eager to show Vinny that she understood.

'Vinny, I know I shouldn't have read the diary and I'm sorry, but I think I understand now, I really do. I really, really do. What can we do? What about Sarina and Abby's older sister – they must be going through the same thing?' Vinny sat down on the bed and sighed heavily.

'I know you understand now, Sofia, I really do. And I want to help too. I've racked my brain and talked to Dad, but he says the only thing we can do is watch Abby, watch all of our friends, stop it happening again. It's weird to think about parents we know, who we like, doing this stuff to their children but it's real alright. And it's definitely not fair.'

Sofia looked sleepy and Vinny felt defeated so they tucked down under their bedcovers and waited for sleep.

Sofia quickly reverted to her ten-year-old ways as she drifted off to sleep, fantasising about rescuing the beautiful Sarina.

The heroic rescue of Sarina would need my genius planning. Yes, I would arrange everything; planes, trains and cars would all be needed.

I would also need access to the internet so I could set up a live rescue mission for the entire web to witness. I would need to take Vinny the swot with me as I would need an assistant to help carry out my master plan...

34

At breakfast time I find out I am right to trust Mum and Dad. Dad has been busy: his first priority has been to establish what the school and the police can do to protect Abby.

'There's good news, Vinny; Abby can be subject to a protection order, to stop her parents taking her out of the country. At least that takes away the immediate danger for Abby.'

I punch the air, 'Yes,' just as the phone rings. It's Abby and she sounds unhappy.

'Hi Abby, you don't sound too good.'

'Oh sorry, Vinny, I'm just not sleeping.' Abby says flatly. 'It's as if around every corner there is a shadow of Uncle Taj ready to take me back. Plus I promised Sarina that I would do something to get her home and I've done nothing.

'I won't ever feel free knowing Dad wants to send me back to get married. I don't trust him enough to get into a car with him let alone anywhere near an airport. Mum supports me now but she has led a very traditional life and isn't always able to stand up to Dad.'

'Do you know what, Abby', I say firmly, 'I think you did the best you could at the time. I could have done something too. If we had only gone to a teacher when it was all being arranged, perhaps Sarina might have talked properly about how she felt, that she was scared, or unsure, then she may have realised what she was really letting herself in for. That's what we should have done for her, way back when we first knew. It might have made a difference. It's too late now for regrets, it's a waste of time. We need to take action not look back. I'm hatching my plan, Abby, more on that soon, I promise.

'And best of all Dad has been on the phone talking to lots of people this week and he says that it is slowly but surely being sorted out. He wants to speak to you, just hang on,' I say, handing the phone to Dad.

'Abby, things are happening. I have spoken to the Foreign Office, the police and Freedom Charity. Freedom will help you get a Forced Marriage Protection Order* which means that you cannot be taken out of the country and if need be they can get your parents to hand over your passport. I have also arranged for you to see a specialist police officer today who will be able to help you.'

Dad continues to reassure Abby and tells her that Jasmine and Vinny will pick her up within the hour. Ten minutes later the doorbell rings and there stands Abby panting and out of breath.

'I couldn't wait, I had to run straight over,' Abby says, trying to catch her breath.

'Come in.' I put my arms around her. 'It's good news isn't it!'

Mum gives us orange juice and cupcakes.

'You will come with me?' Abby says holding my arm.

'Don't worry, Abby, Vinny and Jasmine will both go with you,' says Dad.

Several hours later, Mum and I walk with Abby to the police station.

The police officer introduces herself as PC Jacqueline Williams. She tells us she is a specialist officer in child abduction and forced marriage.

Abby goes in to be interviewed by herself and Mum and I patiently wait in reception.

'Are you okay?' I say rushing to give Abby a hug when she comes out after what seems like hours.

'It wasn't as bad as I thought,' Abby says.

I can tell Abby has been crying as her eyes are bloodshot and puffy.

As we walk back home Abby confides in us after showing me

a special phone she has been given with an App that can trace her and let the police know she is safe.

'Jacqueline, the police officer, was really understanding. She has given me her mobile number and said that I can call her at anytime. She has helped several girls and even a boy in a similar situation to me and Sarina. She said that I could not be forced into a marriage, that I couldn't be forced onto a plane and taken abroad and if I didn't feel safe at home there were other options available,' Abby said without pausing.

'What do you mean?' I quiz.

Abby is looking much happier and seems fit to explode with information.

'Jacqueline had already contacted children's services about me. They could find me somewhere safe to stay and look after me if I wanted that,' Abby says.

'You can stay with us,' I say 'Can't she Mum?'

Mum nods.

'I really want to stay at home,' Abby says.

'I want my Mum and Dad to accept I have the right to decide what I want to do. And I don't want to get married. With the pressure of the law perhaps my Dad won't force me now knowing they're being watched.

'Jacqueline also interviewed me about Sarina and my sister Anna and she thinks they can help but it might take some time.'

As soon as we arrive home we all go to the kitchen to talk further. Dad is waiting for us, eager to find out how it went and also to fill us in on what he's been up to and more. Sofia is safely at next-door-aunty's so we can talk freely.

He tells us that behind the scenes a chain reaction has started. The professional agencies are now in place and aware of Abby and Sarina's plight and are also putting into place measures to bring Sarina back into the UK.

He says that by our actions and bravery we were an important part of the rescue of Sarina and maybe Anna and other victims of forced marriage.

Abby and I smile at each other.

Of course Dad has already spoken to Abby's dad and warned him that he is being watched by the authorities and that he is duty bound to inform the police if anything happens to Abby or if she goes missing.

He tells us that Abby also has Dr Begum onside who has made it clear to Abby's Dad that she had to report that Abby was at risk of being taken abroad against her wishes. She had also contacted the Foreign Office for advice and had reported Abby's abduction.

And we are glad to hear that our school has been busy too. They too have informed Child Protection, and the other agencies.

I take all of this in and am glad to hear it. I have to do more though and as soon as Abby goes home I will begin.

Dad moves the computer into our bedroom giving me time there without Sofia so I can crack on with hatching my plan. A lot is riding on my plan; I need to find a solution not only to get Sarina back but also to give Abby back a guarantee of her freedom. Without that, Abby will always feel she is trapped, scared of what is around the corner.

35

Everyone at school knows about Abby. It's the worst kept secret. Alex even put it up on Facebook.

Abby is so distressed that Mrs Metcalf calls her into her office. She can see from Abby's face that she's been crying again.

Mrs Metcalf has a real skill at getting people to talk, even if they don't want to. She doesn't wait long for Abby to explain what is going on.

'It's awful Miss, everyone at school knows what happened to me. I can just see everyone whispering and talking about me.' Abby's face is pale and her eyes are bloodshot from crying. 'I don't know what to do. I hate the fact everyone is talking about me, you know? I hate being the centre of attention, and the fact I left my cousin Sarina out there. I just feel like I'm failing everyone. I hate coming to school, I hate everything, I wish I was-'

Mrs Metcalf stops her, 'Abby, my dear, you have done absolutely nothing wrong. The way you are feeling is perfectly natural, but you must understand that none of this was in your control. You haven't failed anybody. You mustn't think that.' Mrs Metcalf pauses, 'There is help available for you, in the way of counselling, if you'd be interested. Would you?'

Abby slowly nods.

'Good. I'll call Freedom Charity and we'll sort something out for you. Alright Abby?'

Abby nods again and manages a small smile between tears.

'As for the school gossip trawl, Abby, it will pass, but in the meantime, I will do everything I can to stop it.'

Mrs Metcalf gives Abby some time, and her patience pays off

because Abby stops crying. Abby is reassured by Mrs Metcalf's words and it is not long before she feels ready to go back out and face the rest of her day at school.

When Abby leaves the room Mrs Metcalf phones Jane at Freedom Charity. They discuss Abby's situation and arrange some counselling for her. Jane also thinks it would be a good idea to come in and do an assembly on forced marriage. They both agree that would be a good way to raise awareness to the school of the topic, as well as to help Abby's peers understand her situation a little better and be more sensitive as to how she is feeling.

'Thank you, Jane. I'm sure your coming in will really help.'

The day of the assembly arrives and the whole year is present to learn about the dangers and warning signs of forced marriage. The words 'Freedom2Choose' are projected onto a screen at the front of the room.

You can hear a pin drop, as awful true stories are told about young children being forced to marry; many are much younger than us. Everyone is listening and wants to make a difference and help. Knowing Abby, and the fact that this has happened in our school, brings the situation to life. Alex, Minny, and I are all desperate to help, and when Jane tells us we can save our best friends' lives, I know it's true. It gives me a real sense of power that even though I am not grown up, I can do something.

Mrs Metcalf stands up at the end. 'We have been asked to nominate two or three of you to become ambassadors for Freedom, and peer mentors for the school. If anyone would like to volunteer, please let your form tutor know.'

At lunch, people are talking about the assembly. Mrs Metcalf walks through the hall and, as usual, she stops at tables to sit and chat with her students.

There is an amnesty on our phones for the lunch break, which means we can have the phones switched on to download the Freedom Charity App.

'It's true,' Alex laughs, 'Less boring than a leaflet.' A line he's taken from the short film we have all just watched.

'The App means you are only two clicks away from calling the police or Freedom for help, and it's got all the warning signs,' Minny recites from the assembly.

I'm really interested that the App is not just about forced marriage but all sorts of abuse. I hadn't really thought that making someone marry someone when they don't want to is abuse.

'Abby, have you downloaded the App?' Minny asks, as she munches her apple.

'Mmm yes,' Abby says timidly. She looks embarrassed, knowing she has a lot more than the basic App on her phone. She also has one that Jacqueline, the police officer that is looking after her, has given her.

'Miss, can I talk to you?' Vinny says earnestly. 'I wanted to see if I could be considered to be an ambassador.'

'Vinny, I so hoped you would want to be involved. I think you would be excellent. I will put your name forward. This is a commitment but I'm sure you are up to the job.'

On the way home I call Dad while he's at work and tell him my plans.

'That's great news.' I can hear Dad's smile through his voice.

When I tell Mum, her first reaction is, 'What about your school work?'

'I can do both, honestly Mum,' I insist.

'Yes, but this is an important year and you are so passionate about this.' She pauses. 'But, if you are sure, then we trust you to manage to do both well. We are so proud of you.'

I go into the bedroom and shut the door to start working on a way to get Sarina back.

Sofia bursts in, 'What's up with you, you're always having private time these days,' Sofia complains.

'Please don't start.'

'What's wrong?' Sofia sounding grown up, stares at my computer screen.

'It's Abby, isn't it?' Sofia says.

'Yes,' and I have to say I feel a bit relieved, maybe my little sister will understand. 'Her Dad will send her back over there again if he can to get her married too. And then there's Sarina, she's still trapped out there.'

'Their mum and dad are very different to ours, aren't they?' Sofia sighs.

'Very different, we're pretty lucky, although we don't always know it.'

'Well I expect they nag us all the time about doing our homework because they want us to have a good education so we will have choices for our future,' Sofia says seriously.

'Yes, and if we study and want to go to university we can.'

'Or,' Sofia interrupts giggling, 'to marry a billionaire footballer and never work again, that's okay too.' Sofia smiles hoping I will approve of her amusing answer.

'Imagine Dad's reaction!'

'Hey Sis, I think you've finally got it.' I smile, giving her a hug.

'Well, I think marrying a billionaire is far easier than doing homework any day of the week,' Sofia beams.

I point to the door pretending to be stern. 'Now go, I need to think.'

'Okay Sis, bye.' She skips out.

My mind is racing through other injustices I've heard of, and then it hits me; of course, the media, it's worth a shot. I rush into the living room to tell Dad my plan and he agrees it is a good one and it might just work.

I tear out of the bedroom, dash to Abby's and hammer on the door hoping to make it before she leaves to visit her mum. She laughs when she opens the door, it is a repeat of this morning only with me on her doorstep this time.

'Abby,' I yelp, pulling her outside and closing her front door, 'I've just had a light-bulb moment; I think there is a way. Look

Abby, you leave it with me, you focus on your mum and her recovery and of course you have the kids to deal with. We will get Sarina back and we'll make sure you're safe too, I promise.'

Abby grabs me and gives me a big kiss, 'You're the best friend a girl could ever have, I mean it Vin. I've got to sort the kids' tea out, I'll speak to you later.' Abby goes back inside.

I rush home and begin to type.

36

Saving My Friend by Vinny.

Mine is the guest blog on Freedom Charity's website. Mum and Dad are so proud of me, I can't stop smiling.

'Maybe I could be a journalist,' I think secretly.

Sofia suddenly announces, 'I'm going onto TV to tell everyone about Abby and the others.'

I'm taken aback, I don't know why but I feel myself fighting back the tears. I know this is not all about me. I know it's about Sarina, I know it's about Abby, but I can't understand why it is that Sophia is trying to take it away from me, again. She's always doing this.

'Mum, it's not fair,' I hear myself whine. Mum looks at me and we both start laughing. She holds my hand and squeezes it gently, in the way that only a mum can do. She fetches me a milky coffee.

'It's okay. You know Sofia is just being Sofia. This is really about helping Sarina, trying to get her out, and making sure she never gets taken abroad again.'

'Okay,' I say in a quiet voice. 'I know. I know it's really only about Sarina, and other girls like her and Anna. Sofia just brought everything to the surface.

Later that day I'm taken to the Freedom Charity offices. Mum comes with me. It's really cool. They have a great big white office with big black beams running across the ceilings. Everyone is incredibly friendly and they show me my blog that they have posted. I see it is the guest blog of the day.

Suddenly, I see comments pouring in underneath my blog. People are saying 'Well done,' and asking questions about what to do if they spot the signs of abuse.

They have posted a link to the blog on their Twitter page and there have been lots of retweets. It seems incredible. People are actually interested in forced marriage, how to spot the signs, and how they can help. There are so many girls who have been through the same thing, and we want to make it stop. I'm asked lots of questions in the comments. I'm trying to recall as many things as I can and I ask some of the Freedom Charity workers for help.

Mum gives me some money when we get back from our trip to the Freedom office, to go out for some food with Abby. We go for pizza and I order a bowl of olives as a starter. Abby pushes the plate away.

'I don't think I like them,' she says. 'I don't think they're my thing.'

I push a cocktail stick in an olive and pass it over to Abby, who pulls a face, but takes it anyway.

'They're not as bad as they look,' she smiles.

'I've got a dictaphone on my phone and I'm going to record us. It will save me writing notes.'

Abby rolls her eyes at me. 'You're turning into a journalist,' she sighs, and we are both laughing now.

'This is serious. Having been in to Freedom's office today, they said that one of the most important things is finding out Sarina's address.'

'She's not allowed out of the house at all.' Abby sighs again. She starts to tell me the names of villages and she describes how to walk to Sarina's village from where she was staying with her uncle Taj. She promises that she will try to get me the address from her mum and dad as soon as she gets home.

When I have the address, I phone Freedom and speak to Jane. She is my main point of contact at the charity.

I'm really excited now, because it no longer feels like looking for a needle in a haystack. As long as Sarina is in the same place as she was when Abby saw her, Freedom has reassured me that they will do all they can to ensure she gets back safely.

Jane did warn me though. 'Don't immediately think someone will be flying in James Bond style, jumping out of a helicopter, plucking Sarina away, and bringing her back home.'

I think she is trying to manage my expectations, but the address is a good start, a really good start. It's about opportunities, about finding the right time, and although we'll be desperate for it to happen tomorrow, the rescue has to be planned and co-ordinated. I feel incredibly positive about the whole thing.

The following day, I'm chatting on the phone, but I don't feel as included as when I first gave the address to Jane. Jane tells me I have to trust them to find a solution but it's hard not to be involved all the time. I have to realise that it isn't me who is the important person here.

She reassures me, 'You have to let us get on with our part of the job.'

I know lots of negotiations are going on between Freedom, the Forced Marriage unit, and authorities in the country where Sarina is being held.

Every day I check my phone for a message or text. Every day seems like a lifetime and being back at school seems so pointless. All I want to do is just get on the plane myself. I've got the address and I really wish I could just bring Sarina back. I know it's too dangerous though and I know it would be impossible.

Besides, I have something to think about now, worrying where Sarina will stay when she comes home. It's unlikely she's ever going to want to move back in with her Mum and Dad; even though she loves her family, they left her out there knowing she was so unhappy.

Luckily, things have already been arranged. I got a chance to visit a safe house the last time I went to the Freedom office. It's a lovely house and I've spoken to the young women and girls who live there. They are happy and feel safe after leaving home or being rescued. It is quite far away in the countryside but it's a nice house and everyone's got their own studio apartment. It's like the accommodation I've been to see when I went to a couple of university open days earlier in the year. The room consists of a single bed, a desk, and small bedside table, with a shower room off to the side of the bed. The small kitchen area has a sink, microwave, and a small 2 ring stove. It's got everything Sarina needs. Downstairs, the reception area is secure and no one can get in without going past the security checks. There is also a communal living area with comfy sofas and armchairs, and a large kitchen where a few girls were having a cookery lesson. Some of the women were going off to the local college. Lots of things were going on. In a small hall they had a yoga class, and in another room they were teaching the women how to set up a bank account and manage their money.

Everyone was trying to help and support each other but the most important thing is that the address is not given out to anyone. The women and the girls have to promise not to tell anyone about the place because it would not only put themselves in danger, but everyone else staying there as well. Safety is one of the most important things, I am told by the staff. It is important to me that I see where Sarina will stay when she comes back.

Before Sarina comes back though, Abby wants to post a phone to where she is, as she says it's really important for Sarina to be able to call her friends and tell them what's going on. But everyone thinks it is a bad idea, because what would happen if someone opens Sarina's parcel? She's got absolutely no freedom to do what she wants to. If someone finds a mobile phone in the package, even if it is hidden and wrapped in something else, it really could be more trouble for her.

School is as dull as anything and it all seems so pointless. All I can think about is Sarina and how she's going to be rescued and brought back to the UK. I am constantly staring at my phone, even in school, although we are not supposed to have our phones on, waiting for a message, waiting to hear her voice, waiting to know something has happened.

The minutes turn into hours, and the hours into days. It's been four days now since I've visited the office, since I gave her address to the Freedom team, and still nothing. I contact Jane every day and although I'm sure she must be fed up of me, she is always patient and reassuring. As I'm walking home after spending the last two hours in the library finishing off my project for English, my mobile pings. I look down and there is a text from Jane at Freedom. My heart misses a beat. I feel short of breath as I stare at the screen.

I scream out loud. Everyone stares at me. I am so excited to get home that I run all the way.

I'm so out of breath as I bound into the house.

'She is out!' That's all the text said.

That means Sarina is free, she's been rescued.

Shouting excitedly, I jump onto Mum and Dad, who are sitting on the sofa. I show them the text and we all hug each other. Mum is crying now.

Sofia walks in from Drama club with her new school bag that is almost the same size as her, and it is full to the brim with loads of books. She seems to be taking in all the books that she needs for the whole week, every single day. She says it's just in case the school change the timetable. She is frightened of being caught out. Also, even though she has decorated her locker with lots of pictures of her latest pop and film heroes, she doesn't really want to use it. Plus, she's put her dance kit, her rugby kit, and karate kit in there. Clearly her books are the one thing she does not put in her locker.

As she walks into the room, doubled over, struggling with the weight of her bag, she spots us, shrieks, and asks what's happened. She jumps on top of the sofa and whacks me with her bag.

I scream, and shout 'You bl**dy idiot!' but Mum and Dad are not very pleased with my language and tell me off.

The mood quickly changes though. I explain to Sofia that Sarina is free, and we're all so excited, that no-one can be angry for long.

Then it dawns on me. In all the excitement I have forgotten to tell the one person that needs to know the great news. Abby.

As I grab my phone from Sofia, it rings. It is the Freedom Charity office.

'I've got some fantastic news,' Jane says. 'Sarina is out and they have taken her into a hospital in the city so she can be fully checked out. Then she will be on a flight back to the UK in a few days.'

'That is fantastic news. I will let her cousin Abby know,' I beam.

I call Abby.

'It's Sarina isn't it, what's happened?' she asks in a small voice.

'She's out and they have taken her into hospital just to make sure she is OK.'

I can hear Abby burst into tears at the other end of the phone. I know she still feels guilty for leaving Sarina out there.

'I need to see you, I'm coming over!' Before she can finish the sentence, I know she will be running out the door.

I wait by my own door, and it's not long before I see her running down my street.

'Oh Vinny!' Abby is crying. She is panting loudly and beads of sweat are running down her bright red face.

Mum, Dad, and Sofia are all at the door. There is a moment of silence as the realisation that Sarina is safe sinks in, but we know her journey is just starting.

1 MONTH LATER

BIG NEWS DAY

'Help me with my hair. What shall I wear?' Sofia is in a complete state in the bedroom. 'Darling, you look lovely and to be honest with you, I think the news people will only really want to see Vinny,' Mum says kindly.

The flat is bustling with a camera crew, comprising the cameraman, sound engineer with his big boom, and the Charming Chazza, the famous TV newsreader, the hunk of daytime TV.

As the cameraman is setting up the lighting and rearranging things, Chazza is in our kitchen.

Next-door-aunty suddenly appears with a tray of homemade biscuits and cupcakes that have had a master class in decoration.

'Wow, are they for us?' Sofia asks, eying them greedily.

'No, these are for you, Chazza. I made these especially for you, my dear,' she smiles.

Pleased with the attention, and always happy to meet a fan, Chazza helps himself to a cupcake decorated with red and white icing to match his favourite football team.

He has barely taken a bite before next-door-aunty chimes in. 'Have another one dear, you need to keep your strength up.' She winks and blushes.

Sofia is wearing her black and white striped dress, with its enormous pink bow tied at the back.

'I've always wanted to be a TV presenter like you,' she says, smiling sweetly at Chazza. He starts chatting away, humouring her.

'Come on, let's go in the other room and have some tea,'

Mum says as she ushers everyone out, leaving Vinny to talk to Chazza and the film crew.

Sofia gushes, 'I think he's even more gorgeous in real life.'

'Shh!' everyone interjects.

The interview starts. 'So Vinny... forced marriage,' says Chazza.

I can feel my heart pounding and my palms are clammy. I swallow hard thinking of Abby and Sarina. Dad, Mum and Sofia and Abby are standing nearby and looking at their faces, I find the courage to nod.

* * *

No sooner has the film crew packed and left than next-door-aunty is at the door. We are in the living room impatiently waiting for my three minutes of fame.

Finally it is on:

'So Vinny, your blog 'How to save your best friend's life' has caused quite a stir and you have quite a following now, so tell us, what made you write about forced marriage?'

The camera pans to Vinny.

Sofia screams, 'That's you on telly.'

'Shh,' everyone says at once.

'Well, some dear friends, including my best friend, have been affected. They were taken abroad, one was forced into a marriage, one managed to come back home safely. At first I didn't have a clue about what to do.

'I thought it would help other girls to help their friends if I identified the key things to look out for if you feel your friend is at risk of being forced into a marriage.'

'Vinny, that is great, can you tell us some of them please?' Emma says, smiling at the camera.

After a month of solid researching and blogging I know the signs of a forced marriage off the top of my head so I take a deep breath and rattle them off.

'Well, the key signs to watch out for are:

If your friend seems:
- Anxious
- Depressed
- Emotionally withdrawn with low self esteem

Or if they have a family history of an older brother or sister marrying very young. If their parents are unusually strict and do not allow them to attend after school clubs or classes.

If they start to do any of the following:
- Self harming or developing eating disorders.
- Change of behaviour or challenging behaviour, getting in trouble
- Becoming demotivated and giving up on homework or school

If it seems as if they've given up, or if they are usually active on social media and their Facebook page disappears or is not updated as regularly…

You know something is wrong, so you need to ask your friend what's happening and start doing something about it.

If your suspicions are correct you must talk to a teacher or someone you trust. There are also specialist police officers who can help.

There is also a charity who know all about Forced Marriage, they're called Freedom and they helped us.

If you do nothing and your friend is taken abroad and forced into marrying against their will, you will wish you had done something to help save them, so please act now if you need to. Save your best friend.'

'Well, there is quite a lot there, Vinny, and I am sure people looking at your blog will now know how to save their friend's life. Thank you Vinny and good luck with your blog.'

As the camera pans out Sofia is just seen in the corner of the screen smiling broadly.

'Well done,' everyone says all at once,

Mum cries, 'I am so proud of you.'

'Well, you are a Star!' next-door-aunty says, hugging me.

'Did you see me, right at the end,' Sofia screams excitedly.

'Vinny, look, you have more comments on your blog,' Dad says proudly.

I feel myself going red but I feel quietly proud.

Abby whispers quietly to Vinny, 'I think you are amazing. Thank you.'

'Hey it's not fair,' says Sofia.

'Sofia, what now!' demand Mum and Dad together.

'It's not fair that not everyone has a friend or a sister like you, Vinny.'

'Aah Sofia,' we all shout.

Dear Reader

This is the end of the story and I hope you enjoyed finding out what happened. More importantly, I hope you have learned what you can do if you or your best friend are ever in the position of any of the characters in 'But It's Not Fair'.

I may have met some of you when I visited your school. Hopefully I will meet others of you in the future. In the next few pages, we have some interesting facts and information we hope will be useful should you ever need it. Just remember that you can make a difference. And doing nothing is not an option!

Your friend,
Aneeta
xxx

In the following pages:

- Dear Reader. A letter from the Forced Marriage Unit
- A letter from Sophie, a caseworker in the Forced Marriage Unit
- Advice from commander Mak Chishty, Metropolitan Police Service & ACPO lead
- Warning Signs of Forced Marriage from Anne-Marie Hutchinson
- Help Page. Information on Freedom Charity, their Helpline and the App
- Guidance for Teachers
- Donation information - how you can help
- About the author, Aneeta Prem

Dear Reader,

It can feel like a scary thing to ask for help especially when it's a situation that seems out of your control but the best step is to ask someone you trust for support.

Not talking about the problem does not make it go away; it can then seem bigger and scarier in your head.

Forced marriage is not only a crime, it's an abuse of someone's human rights and can take away a person's right to choose the life they hope and deserve to have.

You may feel as though you are the only one, but you aren't. Thousands of people take the brave step and ask for help. There are many professionals out there specifically trained to put a stop to forced marriage and dishonour based violence.

You or a friend at risk can get help in many ways and you need to remember it's not about getting family or relatives into trouble; it's about being protected from a traumatic situation that you don't deserve to be in.

If you fear that an overseas trip could end up in a forced marriage, think about how you need help.

If you want to go on the trip as you aren't sure if it is definitely for a forced marriage, think about how you can safely stay in touch with friends and professionals, such as a teacher, in the UK. Keep contact options open. Your phone may be taken from you, so check that you have secretly written the key numbers down somewhere. Take down helpline numbers such as Freedom Charity, Forced Marriage Unit and Childline. Before you go, try to get the number for the British Embassy where you will be going and if possible, have a secret mobile phone or sim card.

Give someone in the UK as much information as possible about where you may be going - do you know the address? Set up a code word to text at the beginning of each message so they know it's you and not someone else using your phone, pretending to be you. Create code phrases to state whether things are good or bad...for example, 'it's sunny here' means it's all ok, 'it's cold' means you need help. State when you expect to come back to UK and promise to text or call within 24 hours of being there. The right people can then know what is happening when you are away and if you are in trouble, help can be sought.

If you have a British Passport, staff at a British Embassy can get help for you, may be able to rescue you or find a reason for you to be seen at the Embassy where we can then get you safely back to the UK.

A forced marriage can be a life sentence that no-one deserves. It is in no-one's culture to do this, no religion says it's okay, and it is about power and control. Every person has the right to control their own destiny. We are all here to help a person take that bold step forward in asking for help. We can stop these awful situations and whilst the road ahead can seem challenging, you will supported by so many along the way, you will know you made the right choice and will able to have the freedom to choose how you live your life. You are not alone, help is here.

Forced Marriage Unit

Hello my name is Sophie
(not the same Sophie from this book!)
I'm a caseworker in the Forced Marriage Unit.

When you have the courage to pick up the phone and call
I am here to help. I, like the whole FMU team, want to hear
your story, understand your situation, will be able to give
you options and want to work out a way to help you. At the
FMU we won't judge you, push you to do things you don't
want, but will ensure you are safe and know what your
rights are.

Everyone should have the freedom to choose the life they
want, whether they go to university, travel the world, get
married and have a family or still just want time to figure
out what it is they want.
The Government and organisations like Freedom Charity
are here to support you. The first step in stopping a forced
marriage is asking for help - you are not alone, we are
waiting to assist.

Sophie x

Dear Reader,

My name is Commander Mak Chishty
I am the UK lead on forced marriage and dishonour abuse. If by reading 'But It's Not Fair' you think you could be at risk of being forced into a marriage or being abused, you need to do something about it. You can use the Freedom Charity app, call or text the Freedom Helpline or call the Forced Marriage Unit. But if you believe you are in immediate danger, you need to dial 999. We take every call seriously and we are here to help you. We have worked with Freedom Charity and making this call could save your life or that of your best friend.

Commander Mak Chishty

Metropolitan Police Service (MPS) Association of Chief Police Officers (ACPO)
Lead on Forced Marriage

SIGNS OF FORCED MARRIAGES

No two cases of Forced Marriage are the same and you will know your friends and classmates better than anyone else.

There are signs that may suggest that your friend is in trouble and threatened with a Forced Marriage.

Key signs to look out for:

- Your friend seems anxious and depressed.
- Your friend may appear generally flat and not interested in life. Your friend seems withdrawn and reluctant to talk about what is going on in her family or about her family members.
- Your friend may have told you that some of her/his brothers or sisters have been married at a very young age.
- Your friend may be suffering from mood swings and presenting challenging behaviour and in particular getting into trouble in the school.
- Your friend may be attention seeking.
- Your friend may lose interest in continuing with her education, taking little interest in homework and not seeming to be working towards exam success.
- Your friend's movements may be restricted by family members.
- Your friend may be accompanied to and from school and not allowed to go to after school clubs.
- Your friend may simply not come to school at all but at the same time not have told you that they are ill.
- Your friend may disappear from social networks such as Facebook and instant messaging. Their Facebook may remain not updated for a long period of time.
- Your friend in some cases may start self harming by cutting or develop an eating disorder especially anorexia.

The steps you can take.

If you are worried about a friend who is exhibiting any of the above signs and fear that they may be forced into a marriage, tell your teacher or your school mentor. You can say that you wish to remain anonymous. Tell your teachers that there are specialist police officers who can help. Tell your teachers that there is a Forced Marriage Unit at the Foreign Office. Give your teachers and your school the links and addresses that are in this book.

Many Forced Marriages take place in the school/college holidays. It is often very difficult for a young person to take steps to avoid going on holiday even though they are afraid that something will happen. This may be because they do not feel strong enough to take steps to protect themselves or they do not want to believe their family could do such a thing.

If your friend tells you that they think they may be forced into a marriage when they go abroad on a holiday, make sure they take these steps:-

- Make sure they have a phone or SIM card that works abroad.
- Make sure that they have a specific code so that you know that it is them that is texting or contacting you rather than somebody else using their phone.
- Agree a secret set of words that you know will mean they are in trouble and need help but which no one else will suspect, for example, 'What's happening on Hollyoaks?'.
- Agree on a date by which if they are not back, you have permission to tell a teacher or somebody else in authority about your concerns.
- Before they go, tell them to try to get an address or at least the area of the country they are going to and the names of the family members they are visiting.
- Tell them to leave a note of their passport number and the full names of their parents and any adult siblings with you to keep in a safe place.

- Give them the number of the Forced Marriage Unit and ask them to memorise it.
- Make sure that they have the address of the British Embassy or High Commission in the country they are going to – you can get this from the Forced Marriage Unit or from Freedom Charity.
- Ask them to leave a photograph with you to keep in a safe place. Try to persuade your friend to discuss the concerns that they have about the holiday before they go with an advice worker, police officer, the Forced Marriage Unit or a lawyer.

Anne-Marie Hutchinson, OBE
Specialist lawyer in Children's Rights and Forced Marriage

A Forced Marriage Protection Order is a legal document, issued by a judge, which aims to change the behaviour of anyone who is trying to force you into marriage. It contains legally binding conditions on their behaviour, and if they disobey the order they can be sent to prison for up to two years.

Each Forced Marriage Protection Order is unique, as it is designed to protect you according to your individual circumstances. For example, the court may order a person or persons to hand over another person's passport or reveal where they are. In an emergency, an order can be made to protect a person immediately.

The Freedom app can be downloaded at iTunes for iPhones or Google Play for Android phones and Blackberry World.

I would like to thank Freedom Charity for sponsoring this book and ensuring tens of thousands have been donated to young people.
Aneeta Prem

Help page

I want to empower you to know what to do if someone you know is being forced into marriage and facing fear or violence.

Please go to:
www.freedomcharity.org.uk
You will see in more detail what help is available.

If you are in immediate danger or you know someone who is then please call 999 and ask for the police.

Contact details

If you are affected by any of the issues raised in the book and you need to talk to someone, please call Freedom's 24/7 Helpline on Telephone **0845 607 0133**, or text **4freedom** to **88802** for help and advice. **www.freedomcharity.org.uk**

Foreign and Commonwealth office. Forced Marriage Unit. Telephone: **020 7008 0151** Email: **fmu@fco.gov.uk**

For all media enquiries
www.freedomcharity.org.uk

Alternatively, you can follow us on Twitter '**@FreedomCharity**' or like us on Facebook - '**Facebook/FreedomCharity**'.

GUIDANCE FOR TEACHERS

Full guidance can be found: **http://tinyurl.com/kw3lzm2**

Educational establishments should aim to create an environment where pupils feel it is safe to discuss any worries and concerns they may be facing. Whilst forced marriage may not be part of the curriculum, staff should have an awareness of this issue and how to handle this serious child protection issue sensitively and appropriately.

Students need to know that they will be listened to and their concerns taken seriously.

HOW EDUCATIONAL PROFESSIONALS CAN HELP:

- Signposting where appropriate forced marriage materials on where further support and advice can be accessed.
- Displaying relevant information – for example, Freedom Charity's helpline, the number for Childline and the Forced Marriage Unit.
- Ensuring that a private telephone is made available should students need to seek advice discreetly.
- Educating, informing and where possible, formally training all staff about the issues surrounding forced marriage including the warning signs someone may display, remembering that a pupil may prefer go, for example, to a member of lunchtime support staff.
- Enabling a student to have access to a welfare officer, pastoral tutor, learning mentor or school counsellor.
- Encouraging young people to access appropriate advice, information and support.

WHAT TO DO IF YOU SUSPECT A STUDENT IS BEING FORCED INTO A MARRIAGE:

- Speak to the student immediately and alone.
- Have the talk in a location and manner that does not attract the attention of other students or potential relatives who are also pupils at the school.
- Respect and recognise their wishes.
- Do not minimise their concerns.
- Collect as much information as possible.
- Explain all the options to them.
- Never mediate with family.
- Undertake established risk assessment tool which is recognised by your specific agency, for example, CAADA/DASH.
- Contact a trained specialist, for example the FMU or Freedom Charity, as soon as possible.
- If the person is under the age of 18, refer them to a designated safeguarding officer and activate local safeguarding procedures.
- Establish and agree an effective method of contacting the victim discreetly in the future using a codeword to indentify that it is them.
- Where the risk of harm is significant, consider the need for immediate protection away from the family.

Ensuring a child knows they have made the right choice in telling you their concerns is the most important thing to remember.

FREEDOM CHARITY DONATION PAGE

Have you been moved by the plight of some of the characters in this book? What happens to them is not just a story but to some children, a very real issue. Can you spare some money to help them, no matter how little? Your donations will help Freedom Charity run our crucial 24 hour help line and 24 hour text line which is manned by trained professionals. It is a much needed life line to friends and victims who seek help and advice on issues of dishonour abuse.

We need your help to reach a wider audience and help more children in need. You can help us donate more copies of this book to more pupils in the UK. £2.50 will pay for a copy of this book to be donated.

Your donation will help us to continue our vital work and will help protect the lives of children and young people in the UK. If you would like to find out more information about what we do, please visit our website at **www.freedomcharity.org.uk**

'Donate by BT My Donate' - **'Freedom charity 1139657'**

Many thanks for your support.

ABOUT THE AUTHOR

Aneeta Prem was born and raised within the sound of the London's Bow Bells. Aneeta's family originates from Himachal Pradesh, 'The Land of the Gods.' She is the Founder and Life President of Freedom Charity. She was the first qualified female Black Belt karate instructor in the UK. Aneeta is a Magistrate, chairing adult, family and youth courts. Although based in London, Aneeta escapes to the country with her puppy, Deeva Dog!

You can contact me on Facebook and Twitter @AneetaPrem